D0810690

PAPERBOY

PAPERBOY

ISABELLE HOLLAND

Holiday House ♣ New York

Copyright © 1999 by Isabelle Holland
ALL RIGHTS RESERVED
Printed in the United States of America
FIRST EDITION

Library of Congress Cataloging-in-Publication Data
Holland, Isabelle.
Paperboy / by Isabelle Holland. — 1st ed.
p.   cm.
Summary: In 1881 in New York City, 12-year-old Kevin O'Donnell,
ever conscious of the prejudice against the Irish poor,
struggles to support his sick father and young sister
by working as a messenger for a prominent newspaper but finds
his job threatened when he is falsely accused
of stealing from his employer.
ISBN 0-8234-1422-1
1. Irish Americans—Juvenile fiction.   [1. Irish Americans—
Fiction.   2. Newspapers—Fiction.   3. Prejudices—Fiction.   4. New
York (N.Y.)—Fiction.]   I. Title.
PZ7.H7083Pap   1999
[Fic]—DC21   98-36880
CIP
AC

FOR
REGINA GRIFFIN,
WITH MANY THANKS
I. H.

Kevin O'Donnell stood in front of a ladies' dress store, pretending to cast a critical eye on the lace blouses in the window. But in truth he was carefully watching the reflection of an unsuspecting man piling newspapers—the *Times*, the *Post*, and Kevin's favorite, the *Chronicle*, into a dray. It wouldn't be long now.

Reading newspapers had become Kevin's hobby—though his father felt he'd be better off learning a trade and his sister thought they were only for grown-ups. Most of the papers he read were snatched from dustbins and at least a day old. Sometimes he'd get caught up in a story, only to learn that Part One had been in the previous day's edition. This always sent him scurrying around the dustbins again to see if he could find it. Newspapers showed him a different world from the one he'd always known, a world of important men who did important things, the large world beyond the slum that made up his own world. He yearned to be part of it. At night before he went to sleep he plotted and planned how he might enter it. But in the cold light of day it seemed like wanting to be on the moon.

The man turned his back. It was time. Kevin snatched some copies of the *Chronicle* and tore down the street.

"Come back, you thief!" the man yelled. But Kevin had already turned onto the Bowery.

Two blocks later, he felt safe and slowed down. Although still early, the best place to sell stolen papers was any of the saloons on the Bowery. Even at that hour, some of their customers would be drunk enough not to care whether the papers were stolen or not.

Ducking through a door, Kevin entered McDuffy's Saloon and walked slowly down the bar, casing the customers with an experienced eye. Even though he'd spent the first ten of his twelve years on a farm in Ireland, during the last two in New York he'd learned a great deal about both stealing papers and saloons in what seemed a futile effort to prevent his frail sister and himself from starving.

"Journal, sir?" he asked a man crouched over a pint. "Only a penny."

"Begone wit' ye!" the man said, flinging out his arm.

Kevin went on to the next. "Journal, sir?" he asked.

The man turned. Then he extracted a penny from his pocket. He swayed a little as he took the paper. "Shouldn't you be in school?"

Kevin took the penny. "It's Saturday, sir," he said, and backed away, sure that he'd be gone by the time the tipsy man noticed that it was Friday. Quickly he eyed the rest of the customers. Most of them seemed half asleep. One had his head down on the bar. Experience had taught Kevin not to disturb those. Only one more seemed awake enough to be worth bothering about.

"*Chronicle*, sir?" he asked him, holding out the paper. The man shook his head.

The barman came out from the storeroom behind the bar. "All right. That's enough for today," he said.

Kevin tried two other saloons and managed to sell a few more papers. In the meantime he kept an eye open for any likely customers walking by and also for any policeman who would know the moment he saw him that it was Friday, not Saturday, and that Kevin should indeed be in school.

It wasn't that he minded school. In fact, he secretly liked reading and writing—especially writing, which his mother had encouraged as long as she was alive. "The Irish have great poets and writers, Kevin," she had told him, and often recited verses she had learned at school or at home from her own mother.

But Frank O'Donnell was quick to pooh-pooh school learning and writing. "It's better you learn to farm," he had told his son when they lived in Ireland. Later, as landlords were turning off their land farmers who could not pay their rent, he would add bitterly, "Or a trade."

And now that they were in the United States, the argument continued. Only two nights before, the subject had come up again.

"You're wasting your time, Kev," his father grumbled after coming home to find Kevin buried in the *Chronicle*. "That paper is only for the rich and the politicians they own. I'd rather see you studying for a trade."

Maureen looked up. "What kind of trade, Da?"

"A sensible one, like printing. Or construction or bricklaying. What with all the work on building roads and bridges, you'd always have a job."

Kevin looked at his father over the lowered newspaper. "I'd rather be working on a newspaper."

"But, Kevin," Maureen said. "With all that writing wouldn't you have to stay in school? And you're not always going when you should!" Then, sorry for having said this in front of their father, she put her hand over her mouth.

His father glanced at her. "It's all right, Maureen, I know Kevin isn't always at school. But he's like the rest of us men. He has to work." He looked back at Kevin. "Now listen, boyo. Don't be getting grand ideas—ideas like working on a newspaper—in your head. Learn a trade—any decent trade. Find somebody to take you on as an apprentice, or try for a policeman or fireman. But until then, be staying in school!"

"Yes, Da."

Kevin had learned early that arguing with his father didn't do either of them any good. Once Frank O'Donnell had made up his mind about something, it remained made up. So Kevin did show up at school more often, fitting it around any jobs he could get, since the money their father brought home from whatever work he could find paid only for the rent and some food. Unless Kevin earned a few pennies for extra bread or a bit of cheese or fish, they often went to bed hungry. Yet he kept on reading any papers he could get his hands on, reading everything he could about men who came to New York poor and then became leading citizens important enough to have whatever they did recounted in the newspapers.

His father wasn't the only obstacle to his dream. Kevin learned from bitter experience not to talk about his fondness for reading and writing in front of the other boys. "Look at softie!" they'd scoff when they caught him reading. "What you trying to do? Make up to teacher?"

A man was walking briskly toward Kevin. Likely customers were seldom among those walking briskly, since the latter were nearly always on their way somewhere and had something to do and more than likely had already read the paper. So he could never afterward explain what made him hold out a paper and say, "*Chronicle,* sir? Only a penny."

The tall and well-dressed man stopped and looked closely at him. "Where did you get those papers?" he asked.

As Kevin started to run away, the man reached out and grasped his shoulder. "You stole them, didn't you?"

By this time, the man had hold of both of Kevin's shoulders. Kevin tried to wriggle free and then kicked out, but the man stepped neatly aside.

"No, don't do that." He shook the boy's shoulders. "Well?"

Kevin was strong, but the man was stronger. He stared into the man's cool gray eyes. "Yes," he said defiantly, his mind working furiously. If a policeman came by, he'd have to wrench away somehow.

Dropping the papers, Kevin made a frantic effort to get away. But the man held him firmly. "Now pick up the newspapers," he said when Kevin had finally stopped struggling. The man then loosened his hold.

Kevin again tried to run, but the man gripped the back of his collar. "I said, pick them up."

Unable to escape, Kevin stooped down and retrieved the papers.

"That's my paper you stole," the man said.

Kevin looked up at him. "You mean you work there?"

"I do. I also own it."

Kevin's heart skipped a beat. He took a breath. "Sorry about . . . taking them." He paused and looked up at the man. "Can you give me a job?"

The man stared down at him. "Doing what, pray?"

Kevin wanted to say, writing stories. But he knew the man would just laugh at him. So he said, "A messenger?"

"We don't hire anyone who can't read."

"I can read!" Kevin was indignant.

The man handed him one of the papers. "Read the date, please."

Kevin glanced down at the paper. "Friday, April eighth."

"Hmm. What does the headline say?"

Kevin felt his anger rise. "You still think I can't read!"

"I'm trying to find out. What's the headline?"

By this time a small crowd had gathered. The more people around, Kevin thought, the worse for him. A few were already jeering him.

"Ruddy little thief," one said. "Likely he stole those papers."

"Ought to be in the workhouse—or jail!" another offered.

"Maybe he's hungry," a third pointed out. "Jobs aren't that easy to find."

"Money's hard to come by," a woman said softly. "And he's only a child!"

The tall man seemed unfazed by the comments. "Well, what's the headline?" he said.

Kevin wasn't at all sure he wanted to work for this man, even though he did own his favorite paper. But he decided if he read the headline, maybe the man would let him go. "Two Men Killed Below Bridge," he read. Then added, "It's a dangerous job. Me da was hurt working there."

"You can read." The man sounded surprised. "Why do you steal? Can't you find a job? One after school, of course."

"I've tried," Kevin said. Not expecting the man to believe him, he made another effort to get away.

But the man still held his collar. "Just as a matter of curiosity, was it just chance that you chose the *Chronicle* to steal? Why not the *Herald* or the *Times*?"

"I like the *Chronicle* better," Kevin mumbled.

"Why? Because I caught you today?" He seemed amused.

"The stories about people are better."

"Oh?" There was a hint of sarcasm in the man's voice. "Which *Chronicle* story gave you a better picture than the same one in the other papers?"

Kevin had no trouble thinking of one. "The one about the runaway horse on Broadway, the one that knocked over a stall. The *Chronicle* said what kind of horse it was, how long the man had it, and how much it was hurt. All the other papers just said what harm it'd done and how much it would cost the man."

"Yes, that's true. Roberts, who wrote that story, rather likes horses." The man looked intently at Kevin. "All right. I'll expect to see you tomorrow morning—that's Saturday morning—at eight. Come right after school on school days. At three." He released his hold on Kevin's collar. "All right?"

"How much pay?"

"Three dollars a week."

Kevin had never seen so much money in his working life.

"And we don't hire people who steal."

Kevin glared at him. "I don't—" He stopped, remembering he just had.

"Exactly," the man said. "And please remember it."

As Kevin looked down, the man said, "Well, are you going to show up tomorrow morning?"

At this point Kevin had begun to hate the man and everything he represented—most of all his arrogance. But it was a newspaper job. Even more, Maureen needed the food the money could buy. He took a breath. "Yes," he said. Then, looking into the man's stern, austere face, added slowly, "Sir."

"Please be on time. The address is in the paper," the man said. And walked away.

Kevin ran off home to Mulberry Street. On his way, he bought two buns with his pennies.

The stairs were rickety, some broken, and pieces of the banister were missing. The O'Donnells occupied two small rooms on the top story. Kevin's father, favoring the foot he'd broken working on the bridge, had twice fallen down one of the flights and had to have his foot reset at Bellevue Hospital. "The bloody landlords," he was given to muttering, "don't care what happens to us!" Recently, he'd added more than once, "We should never have left Ireland. I'm telling you, Kevin, it was better there."

But they'd been hungry in Ireland, too. The famine was long over, but the landowner's agent, knowing the landowner wanted the land for grazing his horses, squeezed them harder and harder for rent and, when they couldn't pay one month, forced them off their farm. There was nowhere else they could go. And Ireland was where his mother and his older sister had both died of consumption a few months apart, not long before Kevin, his father, and Maureen had left the small farm his family had lived on for generations.

For Kevin, the trip over had been the nightmare of his life, second only in horror to his mother's and sister's deaths. They could only afford to go steerage, which meant they spent long days and nights huddled in the depths of the ship. There was nowhere to go when they were sick, so they sat or lay in the pitching hold, surrounded by vomit and waste, stifled by the terrible stench.

Once, he had managed to sneak up to an upper deck where the first-class passengers had their cabins and dining room. Before being caught and sent back to the hold, he had walked along the corridors, breathing the fresh air there and on the upper decks. Near the dining room, there was the delicious odor of food ready for lunch.

He'd stood there, transfixed with this view of a world he'd never seen and ravenous with hunger. The difference between the upper decks and the fetid smells and filth below remained for him an unbridgeable gap. But a determination to bridge that gap was born in him then.

"Maureen," Kevin said, running up the last few steps, "I've got a bun here. Do you want it?"

But of course she wasn't there. It was Friday and she would be in school—the parochial school she went to. There hadn't been enough money for both to go, so when his father said, "Kevin, it's better your sister goes with the nuns," Kevin agreed. Secretly he wasn't that unhappy. The nuns were strict and the classes smaller and he couldn't get away with as much as he could in the much rowdier public school.

Sitting at the table in the first room, he ate one of the buns, put the other in the cupboard for Maureen, then decided to go out and see if he could make any more money. His father might have found work today, but he could also be in one of the saloons he sometimes went to when work was scarce, especially for a man who was still lame.

Kevin spent the afternoon looking for any odd job he could find, but came up with nothing. Finally, after walking down Broadway and the side streets, he passed City

Hall Park and arrived at Park Row, known as Newspaper Row, near the Brooklyn Bridge. There he found himself staring at the big sign on one of the buildings to his right: NEW YORK CHRONICLE.

Just looking at it gave Kevin a welter of mixed feelings: anger at the man's arrogance, excitement over the job. Then an idea hit him. He turned and ran north for a few blocks and then east. There was no big sign but he knew that it was the office of the *Irish Times*.

Running up the stairs to the second floor, he knocked on the door marked OFFICE. In a few minutes the door opened.

"Yes?" asked the man who stood in the door.

"Do you have a job?" Kevin asked quickly, before the man could shut the door. And then, as recommendation, "I've been offered a job at the *Chronicle*."

The man grinned. "Ah, have you indeed? Doing what? Polishing their lordships' boots?"

"A messenger, running errands."

"Well, that's grand. Then take the job there. They have more money than we do." And he closed the door in Kevin's face.

The tricky thing, Kevin decided, as he wound his way up the stairs of the tenement, would be telling his father about his new job. It was certainly not the kind of job his father had in mind for him. But his da gave him an opening as they were sitting eating dinner, when he said, "Well, Kev, did you get yourself a job?"

Unable to hide his excitement, Kevin told his father and Maureen about the job.

"Keep an eye out for trouble, Kev," his father said. "I know the cut of him. He'll work the blood out of you and then not pay up."

"He won't do that," Kevin said, deflated.

"Ask himself for a dollar in advance."

"Like as not he'll throw me out," Kevin muttered. But his father might be right. It was worth a try.

At eight the next morning Kevin showed up at the *Chronicle*. He stood for a while admiring the building. Then he ran to the office and said he'd come about the job offered him.

The man who let him in raised his eyebrows and then laughed. "Who offered you a job?"

"A tall man. The *Chronicle* is his paper. And he offered me a job. You can ask him."

"Oh, I don't think I'll bother Mr. Langley with any such nonsense." And he started to shut the door.

But Kevin ran under his arm and into the main office.

"Come back here this minute! Catch him somebody!"

Five or six young men, who were sitting at desks around the room, looked up.

"Go on, catch him!" the first man said, trying to grab Kevin as he darted around the desks.

None of the other men moved.

"He did offer me a job!" Kevin insisted.

"A likely story," the first man sneered.

"Maybe he did," one of the sitting men said.

At that point, the tall, severe man Kevin had stopped in the street came out of an office. "What on earth's going on?"

"You did offer me a job, didn't you?" Kevin said.

"I did. Let him go, Jim. He's telling the truth."

"What kind of job did you offer him?" Jim said, letting him go.

"Messenger. You said we needed one."

"I meant somebody older. Somebody who could read well," Jim protested.

"What makes you think he can't?" the man called Langley said. "Here." He picked up a copy of the *Chronicle* and held it out. "By the way, what's your name?"

"Kevin. Kevin O'Donnell."

"All right, Kevin, read that paragraph, the one there," and he pointed to the lead paragraph in the left column.

Kevin looked at the paragraph. "There have been further delays predicted in the opening of the bridge to Brooklyn. Difficulties in getting the pillars deep into the rock and sand below the river, plus increasing numbers of injuries, have slowed the work."

"Well, I'll be—" Jim said. "Sorry, sir."

Mr. Langley said, "All right, Kevin. Let's get you to work. Jim Martin here is managing editor. You'll be getting most of your orders from him. Jim, where's that package you wanted delivered to the printers?" Jim handed him a large envelope. Langley took it and held it out to Kevin. "Take this up to Fourteenth Street—the address is on the envelope—and come right back. There'll be more stuff to go then. All right?"

Kevin turned the letter over, looking at the address. He summoned his courage. "Me da said I should ask for a dollar in advance."

Jim made a sound. It sounded like a snort. "The nerve!" he said.

Mr. Langley's cool gray eyes looked at Kevin. "You'll get paid once a week, on Saturdays. Next week, if you do your job properly, you'll get three dollars—as I promised."

"How do I know you'll give it to me?" Kevin said.

The man's brows went up. "And how do I know you won't take off with the dollar, if I should give it to you now, and not show up again?"

Kevin stared at him. He so resented the man's manner and his way of talking, different from the people Kevin lived among, it had crossed his mind to take the dollar and not come back. But then he remembered that this was not only a job, but also a job on a newspaper. "I'd not do that!"

There was a pause. "What would you do with it if I gave it to you?"

"Buy bread and a bit of mackerel for me and me sister Maureen."

Another pause. Then the man said, "If you do the job properly today and tomorrow, then I'll advance you a dollar. Now deliver this to Fourteenth Street."

All day Kevin kept rushing around delivering letters and packages. He found the whole process of putting out a paper—the interviewing, writing, copyediting, typesetting, and printing—fascinating.

"I liked your story about the runaway horse," he said to Owen Roberts, who was busy typing.

Roberts looked up at him. "Do you like horses?"

"Yes. Nobody in the other papers said how old the horse was or that it came from Ireland."

Roberts, a man with curly red hair and blue eyes, smiled widely. "That's where you're from, isn't it?"

"Yes. Are you from Ireland? You don't sound like it, but you don't talk like most of the people here, either."

"No, I'm from Wales, from Aberystwyth."

"Do they have many horses there?"

"Yes, some very fine ones, but not as many as in Ireland."

"How long have you worked on the paper?" Kevin asked eagerly. "Did you have to have special training?"

"No. I wrote a lot in school. When I came here, I wanted to be a journalist more than anything, so I kept on trying to get a job until I finally landed one."

"Here? On this paper?"

"No. I started in Boston on the *Eagle,* and then heard about a job here, so I took it."

"Kevin," Jim called from the other side of the office. "Here are some pictures to go uptown. Hurry up."

"You better get going," Roberts said quietly. "He can be tough."

"He doesn't like me," Kevin whispered. "Did I do something wrong?"

"He had somebody else lined up for your job."

"There are eight pictures here," Jim said, as he carefully counted the photographs and put them into a bag. "And that's what they're expecting. *Eight* pictures." He handed Kevin the bag.

His meaning was so obvious, Kevin muttered, "What do you think I'm going to do with them? Steal them?"

The man looked directly at him. "It's been known to happen. Some of the pictures we use are valuable."

"Yeah? How much'd somebody give?"

The man said coldly, "More than you could repay."

Kevin's temper flared. He lightly tossed the bag back on the managing editor's desk. "These photographs are too valuable for the likes of me," he said. "Would you be wanting a police guard?"

"What's going on here?" Mr. Langley said, coming out of his office.

"He thinks I'm going to steal these pictures." Kevin stopped. "As if there's nothing better to steal in New York City!"

"No, he doesn't," Langley said. "Now take the photographs where he told you to." He glanced at the editor.

"Well?" Langley said. "Pick them up, Kevin."

Regretting his outburst, Kevin collected the pictures and took off down the stairs.

Kevin worked hard all Sunday, too. As he was leaving Mr. Langley called him into his office. "Here is the advance you requested."

Kevin was startled. He'd forgotten about it. He took the dollar, then looked up at Langley.

"Well?" Langley said.

"Er—thanks," Kevin said.

"You're welcome," said Mr. Langley, dryly.

When Kevin got home that evening after work, their father wasn't there.

"Da coming home?" he asked Maureen, and then, "What might you be hiding there?"

" 'Tis a kitten, Kev. The Greene Street lads were trying to drown it. I took it when Jim Laughlin and Joe McGiver were having at each other."

"Are you daft? What are we to do with it? Da'll skin us for certain."

Maureen looked at him. Her eyes, large and green in her thin face, always made him think of their mother and were a constant reminder of how Maureen herself had nearly died and how much she needed all the food he and his father could bring home. "But Kevin," she said now, "it's only a wee thing! Remember our cat in Clare? And it caught mice."

It was at that point they heard Frank O'Donnell's steps. He was dragging his foot and it was easy to see he wasn't in a good mood. "What the blazes d'you have there?" he growled.

"It's only a kitten, Da," Maureen said. She looked frightened.

"The nuns told her to take care of it," Kevin improvised hastily.

His father gazed sourly at the scrap of tabby fur. He was behind in his payment to St. Catherine's, and he knew it behooved him to stay in well with the sisters. "I hope the good sisters gave you food for it," he grumbled.

"Ay, a wee drop of milk." And Kevin brought out the small bottle of milk he'd bought on the way home with his dollar.

Frank O'Donnell watched his son pour a little of the milk in a dish. "They should drown it and take it out of its misery."

The kitten lapped up the milk in no time. Then it sneezed, spraying milk over its whiskers, looked around and pranced over to Frank, and pounced on his foot.

He looked down. "The woman in the saloon down on Baxter Street could use a cat. She says the rats and mice there are something fierce."

"It's not big enough yet, Da," Maureen protested.

"It'll not be long here," her father said. It sounded like an order. "And where'll it be doing its business? On the floor, I'll be thinking."

"I'll get a bit of dirt in a box," Maureen said hastily. And then, "And now would you be eating some dinner? And Mrs. Lafferty said they'd pudding left over."

"She's a saint, is Eileen Lafferty. Tim Lafferty's a lucky man." He ate a bite of the ham that Maureen had put on his plate. "Good meat. Did she give you that, too?"

"No, Da. Kevin bought it on the way home."

"And how much were you paying for that, Kevin?"

"Ten cents a slice."

"And where did you get the ten cents? Did Mr. High and Mighty—what's his name?—"

"Mr. Langley," Kevin said.

"Well, did Mr. Langley give you the dollar in advance I told you to ask for?"

"He did indeed," Kevin said.

"Hmm." And then, "I wonder what his game is."

"Maybe he doesn't have one, Da," Maureen said. "Maybe he gave it to Kevin because he's kind."

"Don't talk daft, girl!"

Maureen opened her mouth, but closed it when Kevin shook his head. Something in his father's face made him sure that his father's attitude was rooted in his embarrassment that Kevin was so often the provider of their food.

Kevin woke up at six on Monday. He felt under his pillow for what was left of his dollar. He could buy some bread and maybe half a pound of tea, which would be about twenty-five cents.

Maureen was already up and washing at the sink. The kettle was boiling and by the time he sat down, tea was on.

After breakfast, Maureen got ready for school.

"What are you doing with the kitten, Maureen?" her father asked. His color was bad this morning, as it often was.

Maureen looked at him pleadingly. "You'll not be hurting it, Da, now will ye?"

"Since the sisters think that highly of it, maybe you should be taking it back to them—for good care, I mean, while we're not here to be looking after it."

Maureen looked at Kevin.

"I'll walk with you to school," he said and picked up the kitten.

Maureen whispered, "Oh Kev, you know the nuns didn't give it to me to look after. D'you think it'll be all right here with Da?"

He knew it wouldn't be. He himself wouldn't hesitate to put the kitten out in the street, but then what would he tell Maureen? "Come on," he said, tucking the kitten in his jacket. "We have to go to school."

When they got down to the street, Maureen said, "Sister Teresa says St. Francis was a rare one for the animals." She rubbed the kitten's head. "I'll say an extra prayer to him for the kitten. What do you think we ought to call it?"

"Maybe you should name it Francis after the saint," Kevin said, handing it to her.

"Oh, Kev, they won't let me bring it to school! They'll make me put it out."

"Not even if St. Francis would want them to look after it?"

"Kev! Please!"

"Well, what d'you want *me* to do with it?"

As Kevin watched, Maureen burst into tears and ran off toward St. Catherine's.

He waited until she turned a corner, then put the kitten down on the street and started to walk away. When he saw a large dog lurch toward it, growling, he ran back and snatched it up. What could he do with it? He should be in class by now. Putting the kitten back in his jacket, he turned toward Park Row and the *Chronicle*. He had no idea what Jim or Mr. Langley would say, but it seemed less final than what they'd do in school.

As he came up out of Five Points to the bridge, he stared at the eastern side of City Hall, made golden by the sun on this bright April day. What would happen if he left the kitten as a present for Mayor Grace? He grinned to himself. His father had said that William Grace was a good Democrat and a friend to the working man. But that didn't mean he'd want a kitten.

Kevin stood on the corner for a minute, then made his way to the *Chronicle.*

"What's in your jacket?" Pete, one of the copy editors, said the minute he walked in.

Jim looked up. "What on earth? Leave that downstairs!"

"It'll get killed," Kevin said.

"Well—"

Mr. Langley walked past.

"Tell him we can't have wild animals here, sir," Jim said.

Mr. Langley looked at Kevin. "What animal?"

Kevin glared at Jim. "This one," he said, taking the kitten out of his shirt. Then, as an afterthought, "Sir."

Langley stared at it. "Where did you get it, what's it doing here, and why aren't you in school?"

"Me sister Maureen got it off a couple of boys who were going to kill it and I . . . I brought it here because me da . . . me da—"

"Didn't want it either, I bet," Pete said.

"It doesn't eat much," Kevin pointed out, astonished at his advocacy of the kitten.

Mr. Langley came over and picked up the kitten. It opened its mouth, yawned, and pawed at his sleeve.

"If you take it to the street it'll be dead in half an hour," Pete said. "Best drown it."

"No!" Despite himself, Kevin kept thinking about

the cat his mother had loved but they'd left behind. "There are mice here," he added. "I've heard them. And *rats!*"

"I've heard them, too," Roberts said, looking up from his typewriter. He was watching Kevin with some amusement.

"All right," Mr. Langley said, sounding exasperated. "You may keep it here. I've heard mice, too. But you'll have to feed it and clean up after it." He looked at Kevin. "It had better not be underfoot while it's so small—its eyes are hardly open. You may keep it in that office over there. Nobody's used it since Steve left."

As Kevin was walking over to the room, Langley asked, "What are you going to feed it? It's not old enough to catch mice."

"I gave it a bit of bread and milk last night," Kevin said.

"Go out and get some milk and bring it back. Here's some change. Put the milk in this." He reached over, took a broken saucer off one of the desks, and handed it to Kevin. "And then, please go to school."

Kevin put the kitten in the spare office and, after a moment's thought, put his cap down for it to sleep on. When he got back with the milk, he poured it into the saucer, put it down near the now sleeping kitten, and closed the door.

"I'll expect you shortly after three," Mr. Langley said.

♣ ♣ ♣

When school was over Kevin was accosted by Tommy Meehan. "There's gonna be a fight with the Greene Street Boys, Kev. Wanna come?"

Kevin thought longingly of exchanging blows with the Greene Street Boys. His lot, the Mulberry Street Boys, and the boys from Greene Street had been enemies since he could remember.

But he shook his head. "Can't. Got to go to work."

"Who'd be so daft as to hire you?"

"I'll have you know that I am employed by the mighty *Chronicle*."

"That paper that hates the Irish?"

"You got it all wrong, Tommy."

"Didn't you read it this morning? Your own paper?"

" 'Course I did," Kevin said.

"Well, what do you think it means when the paper said the Irish are layabouts, who like stealing better than working? Me da told me about it."

"It's a lie!" Kevin said. He hadn't had a chance to see the paper yet, but he was certainly not going to let on.

As soon as he reached the *Chronicle* office he looked through the paper. And there, in a column on the second to last page, was the headline, "Irish Layabouts."

"It's a lie," he said aloud.

Jim turned away from the desk. "What is?"

"What it says here about the Irish being layabouts."

"Did you read the whole piece?"

"I don't have to read it to know it's a lie."

"It's a good idea to know what you're talking about before you make a fool of yourself."

Kevin stared at him. But Jim had turned back to his desk and was tapping away at one of the typewriters.

Ten minutes later Kevin knew what Jim had meant. Under the headline was a story about a City Hall official who had called the Irish layabouts and shortly thereafter found himself without a job.

Serves him right, Kevin thought.

"Kevin!" Mr. Langley's voice sounded from his office.

Kevin dropped the paper and went to the boss's office. "Yes . . . sir?" The "sir" always came hard.

To his astonishment, Kevin found not only his boss in the office, but the kitten, sound asleep on a pile of papers in the corner.

"What's he doin' here . . . sir?"

"He was meowing his head off, so I brought him in to keep him quiet. He drank the rest of the milk."

Kevin went over and ran his finger down the kitten's back. "He's purring," he said.

"So you like animals?"

"Ay. Me ma had a cat back in Ireland, and I had a dog. But he got off the farm one day and the landlord's agent shot him. Then me ma died and we had to leave the cat when we came here."

"I heard you outside yelling at Jim. What was that about?"

"A friend of mine—Tommy Meehan—said this paper was against the Irish and called them layabouts."

"The story about Councilman Brown."

"Yes."

"Did you read it?"

"Yes . . . yes, sir."

"Then you know it had nothing to do with the *Chronicle*."

"Yes."

"I have a letter for my wife. I want her to get it as soon as possible. Here!"

Kevin took the letter. On the front the address read: "Twelve Washington Square North."

Kevin had been to Washington Square before. He remembered it fondly as a place of grand houses and carriages with handsome horses.

"You know where it is?" Langley asked.

"Yes."

"There'll be an answer, so please wait for it and bring it back right away. This is about plans concerning this evening. And you'd better bring milk back for the cat. Here's some change."

"Yes, sir."

It was a bright spring day. Green shoots were showing on the branches of the trees in the square. Kevin walked up the eastern side of the square and watched the glossy horses pulling their carriages, their hooves making a clop-clop noise on the street.

Number twelve was between Fifth Avenue and University Place. Kevin stared up at it, at the clean windows and the curtains visible behind the panes of glass and thought of his father's words, "the rich and high and mighty." As he put his hand on the gate, he also remembered the top deck of the ship coming over, with its fresh wind and the delicious smell from the dining room. Then he opened the gate, went up the steps, and pulled the bell beside the front door.

In a minute a young woman wearing a white cap and frilled apron opened the door. She looked Kevin up and down. Then her freckled face broke into a grin. "And who would you be?" she asked.

Hearing the Irish in her voice, he grinned back, "I work for Mr. Langley down at the paper, and I have a letter for Mrs. Langley. It's from her husband," he said.

She held out her hand. "Give me the letter."

Kevin held it out. "I'm to wait for an answer."

"Just a minute." She took the letter. "Wait here."

Kevin stood there a minute, then turned and watched the people walking in the square, and the children playing there.

The door behind him opened again. "Mrs. Langley says you're to come inside and wait. She's going to write an answer for you to take back." She held the door open.

Kevin walked into a hallway. Through a door on the left was the largest room he'd ever seen. The ceilings in both the hall and the room seemed immensely high. The furniture shone and there were flowers in the hall and more in the room. Straight ahead were stairs of polished wood going up to the next flight. The air smelled of flowers and another rather pleasant odor.

Kevin sniffed. "What's that smell?"

"Flowers," the maid said.

"No. I can tell those. Another smell."

"Likely furniture polish."

Impressions jumbled together in his head. Here there was no stench from the gutters and open sewers outside as there was down where he lived. This was that other world, the world of the upper deck. He felt his heart beat a little faster.

"Sit here," the maid said. "And take off your cap."

He pulled his cap off, revealing tousled reddish brown hair. "Are you from Clare?" he asked.

She smiled a little. "No. From Mayo." Then she turned and walked away.

"What are Clare and Mayo?" a voice asked.

Kevin turned. A girl, a little younger than himself, was coming down the stairs. In one arm she was cradling a gray-and-white rabbit.

"They're counties in Ireland."

The girl came and stood in front of him. She had light brown hair pulled back with a blue ribbon and gray eyes. Her dress was blue. "My name's Elizabeth. What's yours?"

"Kevin. Kevin O'Donnell."

"How do you do, Kevin," she said. "And this is Bunny. I got him for Easter." Then, as someone came through the front door behind Kevin, "And this is my brother, Christopher."

Kevin turned and saw a slight, fair-haired boy, taller and a little older than himself, taking off his cap. Under his arm he was carrying a book.

"Chris," Elizabeth said, "this is Kevin. He brought a message from Papa."

"Hello," Christopher said. And then, with some curiosity, "Do you work at the paper?"

"Yes," Kevin said.

"What do you do?"

"I'm a messenger. Your da sent me up here with a note for Mrs. Langley."

"Da?" Christopher asked.

"Chris!" Elizabeth said. "You know that means father. Bridie uses it all the time."

"Oh." Her brother seemed to lose interest.

"Did Papa send any message for us?" Elizabeth asked.

Kevin shook his head. "No."

Her brother shrugged. "Did you expect him to? You know, Lizzie, when he's down at the paper, that's all he thinks about."

"That's not true! I'm sure he thinks about us! You know how often—"

But at that moment, a tall lady with dark brown hair piled up on her head came down the stairs, her skirts brushing against the rug. In one hand was an envelope. She addressed her children. "Is this your father's messenger?" she asked.

"Yes, Mama," Elizabeth said. "His name is Kevin."

"Really?" Mrs. Langley sounded completely uninterested.

Kevin's cheeks flushed.

She held out the envelope to him. "Please take this down to the paper as quickly as you can. My husband must have it before he makes his arrangements for this evening."

"Yes, ma'am." Kevin took it and turned toward the door.

"Oh, and, boy, please take this."

Kevin looked back. She was holding out a coin to him, but her face was turned away.

Kevin was astonished to hear himself say, "That won't be needed, ma'am. Mr. Langley pays me at the end of the week."

He shoved his cap on his head and opened the front door. He couldn't believe what he'd just done. How much bread or milk could he have bought with whatever Mrs. Langley was holding out?

Quickly he ran down the steps and started toward the square, his heart beating rapidly. He'd only gone a few yards when he heard the front door of the house open.

"Good-bye, Kevin," Elizabeth's voice called. "Bunny says good-bye."

Slowing, Kevin turned and saw Elizabeth, standing in the door, being pulled back by her mother.

He wanted to ignore her, but couldn't. "Bye."

The kitten was chasing a rolled-up piece of paper in Mr. Langley's office when Kevin got back and handed Mr. Langley his wife's letter.

"Thanks," Mr. Langley said. "Now Jim has some things he'd like you to pick up."

♣ ♣ ♣

The next Saturday Kevin was sitting in the office at eight, reading the paper, waiting for his first instruction of the day. Suddenly, he looked up to see Mr. Langley standing there, holding out three dollars. "Here's your pay, Kevin," he said.

Kevin took the money. "Thanks." Out of his mouth popped the words, "But you gave me one dollar already." Then he sat back, surprised at his own stupidity.

Mr. Langley smiled. "I commend you for telling me that. I'd forgotten." There was a pause. "You've done a fine job. You may keep the extra dollar. You've earned it."

"Thank you, sir," Kevin mumbled. The words still didn't come easily.

"By the way, I heard you met Elizabeth and Christopher. Elizabeth told me."

Wondering what was coming next, Kevin nodded.

For a minute Langley didn't say anything. Then he said, "I sometimes wish Christopher would take more of an interest in the paper. God knows, he likes to read and study!" For a minute he stood there, turning over the sheets of that day's paper. "But, I don't suppose there's anything I can do. Oh well—" And he went back to his office.

"Timmins was here," Maureen told Kevin the next night when he got home from work. Timmins was their landlord and Frank O'Donnell was well behind in his rent.

While their tenement was dirty and broken down, they both knew it was better than the streets.

"What did he want?" Kevin asked.

"The rent," Maureen said. "Has Da given you any money for it?"

"No," Kevin said.

At that moment they heard their father coming up the steps slowly. When Frank O'Donnell got to the top, they both asked at once, "Have you got the rent, Da?"

"If I had the rent, wouldn't I have given it to Timmins?"

"But you have a job, Da, don't you?" Maureen said.

"Ay, I do now. I got hired on the docks yesterday. But there won't be any pay for a week at least."

"You all right, Da?" Kevin asked. His father's face was almost gray and looked drawn.

"Ay. But I'll just sit down for a minute. That job, the pay's good, but there's a lot of lifting and hauling. The man said if I couldn't keep up, they'd hire somebody younger."

As Kevin knew, it was always a threat. "You'll be all right." But he wasn't sure he would be. Da was thirty-nine, but he looked much older.

They were just sitting down to a supper of boiled potatoes, cabbage, carrots, and a bit of meat when there was a banging on the door.

"I've come to get the rent."

Frank put his hands to his lips and shook his head. They both knew what he meant, because it was a tactic he'd used before.

"I know you're in there. Now open the door!"

Frank shook his head at them and they sat still and silent. They knew Timmins couldn't get in, because one purchase Frank had willingly made was a new lock for just this kind of emergency. They'd had to move twice before when Frank couldn't pay the rent, and he was wise to the ways of landlords and how to avoid them.

"All right," the landlord bellowed. "But if I don't have the rent—and the back rent—by the end of the month, then I'll get the cops and you and your family will be out."

After they heard the landlord's steps reach the bottom of the staircase, Frank said, "Kevin, you got any of your pay left?"

"Here, Da." Kevin gave him his two dollars and a little change. He'd planned to buy milk for the kitten, but this was more important. "What'll you do, Da? Ask the boss for some pay in advance?" One look at his father's face gave him the answer to that.

"Ah, Kevin, there are twenty men—younger men—behind me ready to take the job." He paused. "But I'll find it somehow. There's Tommy O'Hare down at the Democratic Club. He might do a man a favor."

"Then you'll have to vote for them," Maureen said. "Won't you, Da?"

"And who else would I be voting for, miss?"

The next day Gerald Lavin, a friend of his father's, stopped Kevin as he came out of school on his way to the paper. "Kevin, your da had a bad accident. What with his foot, he didn't move fast enough, and one of the loads coming off the ship dropped on him."

Kevin felt his heart jump and then miss a beat. "Is he—is he—"

"The lads got him to Bellevue. He's there now. You'd better go there and see him. I know he'd want to talk to you."

But when Kevin got up to the hospital, he found his father in no condition to talk. He was lying in bed, his eyes closed, his face a yellowish gray.

"Da?" Kevin said, standing beside his bed.

Frank's eyes opened, but they were cloudy and unfocused.

"I'm sorry," the doctor said, coming up behind Kevin. "Your father's accident was followed by a heart seizure. I'm afraid it'll be a while before you can talk to him."

Kevin felt as though a hand were squeezing his own heart. He looked down at his father. "Will he be all right?"

"We hope so."

Kevin stood there for a moment, then turned to go.

"Kevin?" The voice was hoarse.

Kevin went back. "Da?"

His father was breathing noisily.

"The doctor said you've been hurt bad," Kevin said.

There was a pause as the heavy breathing continued.

Then Frank whispered, "Kevin, look after Maureen."

Because he'd gone to Bellevue, Kevin knew he'd be late for work. But still he hesitated. Maureen had to be told before she heard it when she got home. And she'd hear, because everybody on Mulberry Street would know.

Making up his mind suddenly, he started running south toward St. Catherine's. He ran for a while, then stopped and puffed, then ran and walked alternatively till he found himself standing on Grand Street, staring east to the docks. Masts rose above the buildings and warehouses, men rolled barrels from the docks to the drays, and huge, patient horses waited for their loads.

Kevin, remembering how his father used to talk about horses in Ireland, found tears running down his cheeks. "They've grand horses, Kevin, the best in the world."

Kevin knew his father wasn't talking about the great shire horses with fringe around their hooves, but he couldn't stop himself from crying, something he hadn't done since his mother and older sister died. Now he was afraid his father would die.

How would he and Maureen manage? Timmins wanted rent and back rent before the end of the month. And what if he came to collect it and nobody was there to pay him the money? Kevin knew Timmins'd think nothing of forcing the door open and throwing what little they owned out on the street. It had happened to others in the building.

Suddenly he was afraid. There were terrible stories about what happened to orphans. A lot of them were split up and sent all the way across the country. He didn't worry too much about himself. He could always find a corner somewhere to sleep. But what about Maureen? If Da died, would the nuns let Maureen live with them? He knew the answer was no. Maureen said they often talked about how crowded the convent was. They might both be sent to the Idiots' and Children's Hospital on Randalls Island far up in the East River. And what would happen to his job then—that is, if they let him keep his job?

But he and Maureen weren't orphans yet, he reassured himself. Da wasn't dead. And nothing must happen to send Maureen away. But there was no question that feeding—and paying rent—for them both was now up to him.

Kevin started running again and finally reached the parochial school. He saw his sister standing with her friends, Eileen McCormick and Mary Lafferty.

"Kevin, why aren't you at work?" She looked at his face. "What's happened?"

He took her hand and pulled her aside. "Da was hurt at the job," he said. "Hurt bad. They took him to Bellevue."

Maureen stared for a minute. Then her face crumpled. "Oh Kevin, is he dead?"

"No, Maureen, no! But the doctor said—"

Maureen took hold of his coat. "Will he die, Kev? Is that what the doctor said?"

"No, Maureen! Now don't get yourself upset! But, well, he'll be ill for a while."

She was holding his jacket with both hands and was crying into it. Feeling awkward, he patted her back. "Now don't take on," he said. "And get off home. I have to go to work."

"But what're we going to do about Mr. Timmins? He's coming for the rent."

"I'll get it," Kevin said, not knowing exactly how he was going to do it, but knowing he must.

"Oh, Kevin, will you?"

"Yes. Now be going off home."

Maureen wiped her eyes with her sleeve. Just as Kevin was walking away she said, "Kev, is the kitten all right? They haven't made you put it out?"

He thought of the kitten asleep in the boss's office. "It's fine," he said.

"Are you coming, Maureen?" one of her friends called.

"Here." Kevin took two coins out of his pocket. "Get a bun and some milk."

"I could light a candle," Maureen said sadly.

"Ay, do that."

Fifteen minutes later he walked into the *Chronicle* office.

"Where've you been?" Jim Martin said coldly. "The boss was looking for you."

Mr. Langley appeared in the doorway. "Come in here, Kevin."

Kevin followed him into his office.

"You're late. What happened to you?"

Kevin hesitated.

"Well?"

There seemed no way out. Kevin blurted out, "Me da had an accident at his job at the docks. He's in the hospital."

"I see." Mr. Langley paused. "What happened to him?"

"A load coming down from the ship fell on him. Hit his head." Kevin paused, then blurted out. "The doctor said he had a—a heart seizure as well."

"What hospital?"

"Bellevue."

"Where's your mother?"

"She's dead. She died in Ireland before we came here."

"Yes. I remember now. Is there anybody else?"

"Me sister, Maureen."

"Umm. How old is she?"

"Ten."

At that point the kitten walked out from behind a pile of newspapers on the table. Kevin eyed it. He'd forgotten to bring any milk. "I forgot the milk," he said.

"You also forgot to bring some dirt. It had done its business all over the floor when I got in this morning. The place smelled vile. But— Well, go and get the dirt now and see to it that it's always there. And empty it every day. Mice or no mice, I'm not sure how long we can keep it here, anyway. Go and get the dirt."

Kevin ran downstairs. He found a box in the garbage outside some vegetable stalls and went across the street to City Hall Park. After digging up some of the dirt there, he slapped it in the box and took off across the street to the *Chronicle*.

"What are we going to do, Kev?" Maureen said that evening. She sounded frightened.

"We'll manage," Kevin said. He didn't know how, but he didn't want to say so. He'd brought home some milk, a little meat, and some bread, which they'd had for dinner. By this time the neighbors had heard about their father's accident. Mrs. Lafferty brought by some pudding and Mrs. O'Boyle some potatoes. "We'll try and save you as much as we can," Mrs. Lafferty said. "Have you told Father Martin yet? He might be able to get some more food for you and Maureen."

"No, not yet," Kevin mumbled. He didn't want to say so, but he knew Father Martin had his eye on him to be an altar boy so he tried to avoid him. I'm too busy, Kevin told himself.

"If Timmins hears about your da you'll be out," Mrs. O'Boyle said, when she came with the potatoes.

"You'll not be telling him?" Kevin pleaded.

"No, but you know how it is down here. I'll not, but somebody will. Then he'll get hold of a policeman or some politician and say it's against the law for two children to live alone."

The next day he decided not to go to school, but to get another job during the day. It wouldn't be hard, he told himself. There were kids working for the garment industry, pulling threads or cleaning up.

But when he asked around, he was told that the pay was maybe a dollar a day for a ten- or twelve-hour day and he didn't want to stop working at the paper.

"Anyway, it's mostly kids that are Italians or Jews," Tommy Meehan said. "I don't think they have any Irish kids doing it. Why don't you see if they have any jobs at the market or in a saloon?"

He was walking on Hester Street the next day when he saw a man sitting in a shop, sewing. The man wore a little round hat on his head and had a long beard.

Kevin paused. "Got any jobs?" he asked.

The man looked him up and down. "What can you do?"

"I can run messages."

"Can you sew?"

"'Course not. That's not work for a man."

"No? Most of the tailors dressing the fine gentlemen uptown are men. Or didn't you know?"

"No. Sorry." Kevin turned and started to walk out.

"I thought you wanted a job."

Kevin turned back. He smiled a little. "You're right about that. Have you got something?"

The man held out a letter. "If you deliver this and bring me back an answer in an hour, I'll give you a nickel."

It wasn't much, but it'd buy something. "All right." He walked toward the man.

The man hesitated, then handed him a letter. "Don't lose it."

"Why'd I do that?"

The man stared at him for a minute. "How old are you?"

"Twelve."

"You look older. Maybe because you're taller than most boys your age. All right. Can you read the address?"

"'Course I can." Kevin glanced down at the envelope. "'Solomon Levine. Twenty Duane Street.'"

"Do you know where Duane Street is?"

Kevin waved toward his right. "That way, about ten blocks down, the other side of Broadway."

"I'll see you back in half an hour."

As Kevin ran off, he found himself wondering what was in the envelope. Stopping, he felt it. The envelope wasn't thick, but it had several sheets of paper in it. He held the envelope up to the sun to see if he could see through it.

While walking along Canal Street, he passed a bunch of boys standing in an alley. "Well, look at the boyo!" one of them said. "What's that you're carrying?" The boy, who was taller than Kevin, strolled forward, followed by one or two other boys. "What's in that letter? Money?"

Kevin started backing off. "There's no money! It's only a letter!"

"Don't you know your commandments? Thou shalt not tell a lie." The boy's hand shot out.

Kevin took off. But he wasn't fast enough. When they caught up with him they snatched the letter from him and tore it open.

Pages covered with a strange-looking script fell out onto the muddy street.

"What's this?" The gang leader said. He stooped and picked up one of the sheets.

"Give me that!" Kevin made a grab at it.

"That's Jew-writing," one of the boys said. "You can see it over the shops on Orchard Street."

"There's no money in it," the leader said disgustedly. He started to tear the sheets across.

Kevin made a lunge at him and managed to knock the sheets out of his hand. The next thing he knew he was lying flat on the sidewalk. He managed to get up and land a punch on the leader's nose, but was grabbed from behind and held while the leader pummeled him. At that moment a policeman came around the corner and the gang fled.

"You're a right mess," the policeman said to Kevin, who was trying to wipe away the blood pouring out of his nose. "What's this?" He bent and picked up the crumpled sheets of paper.

"It's a letter. I was delivering it," Kevin mumbled through his swollen lip.

"Well . . . " The policeman tried to smooth out the muddy sheets. "You'd better take it back to the man who wrote it. He might want to write another one." He handed him the letter and stood watching while Kevin walked to the end of the block.

When Kevin got back to the Hester Street shop, he hesitated, then went in. The man was still sitting sewing. "Well, did you deliver it?"

Kevin held it out. "I got jumped by some kids who thought there was money in it. It got some mud on it. Do you want me to take it, or do you want to write another one?"

The man looked up. "I should never have trusted it to you."

"I can't help it if some bully boys jumped me."

"Bring it here."

When Kevin went forward, the man frowned and said, "You got beat up, didn't you? You were standing with your back to the light, so I didn't see at first." He paused. "Are you all right?"

Touched, despite himself, Kevin nodded.

The man smoothed the letter with his hand and with a cloth wiped the mud off the sheets. Then leaning over, he picked up an iron from a small stove. He tested the bottom with his finger, put the iron down, opened the letter, spread open the sheets, and ironed them quickly on a board nearby.

When the sheets were back in the envelope, he handed them to Kevin. "Now you can deliver it."

Kevin hesitated, but he could almost feel his father pushing him. "What about my nickel?"

"That is for when you come back with the answer." The man looked at him severely. "And don't get into any more fights."

A half hour later Kevin was back with the answer and handed it over. The man put a coin in his hand. It didn't feel like a nickel, more like a penny. About to protest, Kevin looked down and stopped. In his hand was a dime.

When Kevin arrived at the *Chronicle* the next day, he found the office in an uproar.

"But he always writes the editorials," Roberts was saying to Jim.

"And he's the one who decides the story lineup and the features," Jim added.

"What's going on?" Kevin asked.

Roberts looked at him. "The boss broke his leg. He can't come up here with all the stairs, and he's always run the paper pretty much himself. The *Chronicle's* a one-man show."

Kevin stared in shock. To him, Mr. Langley seemed indestructible. "How'd he break his leg?"

"A runaway horse," Roberts said. "The boss was crossing the square last night when a horse knocked him down and then he was hit by the carriage behind." He paused. "What a mess!" He looked at Kevin. "It's going to keep you busy carrying stories back and forth. We can't use the telephone or telegraph for everything. So get ready to take some stories up to the square and bring back what he's been working on."

"He's been working—with a broken leg?"

Roberts smiled a little. "It hasn't hurt his brain. Just his leg."

Kevin thought for a moment. "But there are steps up to his house. How'd he get up?"

"The ambulance from the hospital took him back home after they'd set his leg. I think he's using one of the downstairs rooms for the time being."

Kevin took a trolley up Broadway to West Fourth Street, then walked as quickly as he could to Washington Square. Over his shoulder he carried a bag containing stories for Mr. Langley to check and pages of questions and suggestions from Roberts, Jim, Pete, and a copy of that day's paper. "Although the boss's sure to have sent somebody out to get him a copy," Roberts had said. He then looked at Kevin and smiled. "Now you better get up there."

Bridie opened the door.

"I've brought stuff from the paper for Mr. Langley," Kevin said.

Bridie opened the door wider. "Come in. Mr. Langley's expecting you."

As Kevin took off his cap and followed her through the hall, he was aware again of the size and grace and quiet of the house and the delightful scent of flowers and polish. He was shown into a room at the back, where he saw Mr. Langley, his leg in a plaster cast, sitting on what looked like part bed and part sofa, a cushion under his knee.

Langley looked up. "Come in, Kevin. What have you brought me?"

Kevin walked over and handed him the bag he'd carried.

Langley pulled the papers from the bag. "Sit down while I look through these."

"Roberts said you broke your leg, sir. I'm sorry."

"Yes, the tibia, one of the lower bones. Not as bad as it might have been. But I have to stay off it for a couple of weeks."

Kevin strolled over to the window and stared out. Immediately below the window was an iron balcony with the steps going down to the garden below. Grass, smooth and green, covered most of it, but there were flower beds on either side and in a round spot in the middle. Kevin hadn't seen flowers and grass like that since he'd left Ireland.

"That's a lovely garden you have, sir," he said, almost to himself.

Mr. Langley looked up. "You like gardens? Do you have one—" He stopped, as though suddenly realizing what a foolish question it was.

Kevin turned. "'Course not. But the grass out there is almost as green as in Ireland."

Langley continued looking at him. "How long ago did you come here?"

"Two years ago."

"I think you said your mother died in Ireland."

"Ay. She had the sickness."

Langley paused. "I guess you mean consumption. A lot of your fellow Irish have it." He glanced at the door when it opened. "Oh, hello, Christopher. Have you met Kevin O'Donnell? He's brought me work from the office."

"Yes, Papa, I met Kevin when he brought that letter about the Knickerbocker Ball."

Langley was examining some of the papers Kevin had brought. "Well, right now Kevin and I have to do some work for the *Chronicle,* so don't let us keep you. Now, Kevin, about this placing of the stories. Tell Jim I want the editorial about the survey of city hospitals on page one. The story about the battles going on in City Hall can go on page three. It isn't as though there was anything new about it."

"Papa," Christopher said.

"But I thought editorials always went on the last page of the first section," Kevin said.

"Most of the time, yes. But when something's really important, we put it on the front page."

"Papa!"

"Yes, Christopher, what is it? Can't you see we're busy?"

Christopher glanced at Kevin and flushed. "About the dinner tonight, Mama said—"

"We can discuss that later. Now please—" He stopped as Elizabeth appeared in the doorway next to her brother. "Good afternoon, Elizabeth."

"May I come in?" Elizabeth looked shyly at Kevin. "Hello, Kevin." Then she walked over to her father's couch and kissed him on the cheek. "How are you, Papa?"

"Fine, Elizabeth. It's just my blasted leg. The rest of me's all right. How was school?"

She wrinkled her nose. "The teacher's cross with us. She says we don't do our homework."

Langley looked affectionately at his daughter. "Well, did you do yours?" It seemed to Kevin that Langley liked his daughter better than he did his son.

She giggled. "I like history—at least some of it. I read about the Crusades and the kings of England and I loved them because they were good stories. But I thought the part about the Revolutionary Age was boring."

"You shouldn't. After all, our own Revolution was part of that. Wasn't it, Kevin?"

"Yes. I guess so." He paused. "They don't have anything in my school about Irish history."

"No, they don't," Elizabeth agreed.

Mr. Langley looked at Kevin. "So why don't you tell them?"

"They wouldn't listen. I've tried."

"They really don't listen, Papa," Elizabeth said. "They say we're only children."

He sighed, "You're probably right. Now—you and Christopher are going to have to leave for a while so Kevin and I can get some work done. I'll see you later."

Elizabeth directed a smile at Kevin as she left the room. "'Bye," she said shyly.

"May I do anything, Papa?" Christopher said.

"No." His father said, his eyes back on the papers. "Just leave us."

For a moment Christopher stared at Kevin, unsmiling, then turned away.

Langley spent the next half hour explaining the papers he was handing Kevin, and what he wanted done with them. "This piece about the schools should go in the first section," he said.

Kevin opened his mouth, then shut it again.

Langley glanced at him. "Well?"

"I thought it'd be in the Metropolitan Section," Kevin said.

"Why?"

"Because of the cartoons there. Kids look at them. And if they saw an article about how the schools ought to be better, then they might tell their parents."

Langley looked at him. "You're implying the parents wouldn't get that far themselves." He laughed. "Well, you may have a point. I'll put it in on the front page of the Metropolitan Section. That's a better place for it anyway." He reshuffled the papers, glanced briefly at Kevin, and then away.

At the end of the day, he put the papers in the bag Kevin had brought in. "All right. I think that covers everything. You're going to have to come back here every day until I can manage the stairs down there."

The next day, while his boss was working on some papers, Kevin leaned against the window and stared out at the garden. The trees were thick and green, and the flowers along the walls were in full bloom—bright red and yellow and blue.

At that moment he knew with absolute certainty that what he wanted to do when he grew up was to own—or at least be managing editor or a top reporter on—a newspaper like the *Chronicle* and live in a house on the square with a garden like this. The thought hadn't been in his mind more than a few seconds when he could hear his da's voice, "And where will you be getting the money, Kevin? Do you think their lordships are going to hand it to you? Don't be daft! You know what Father Martin reads from the holy scriptures sometimes? 'To them that hath shall be given.' Well, the Langleys have plenty, so more will be given them. But not to the likes of us." It was a sentiment Da had often expressed before.

A sense of frustration settled on Kevin. But Da hadn't been right about Mr. Langley. He had paid him when he said he would and had let him keep the extra dollar.

It was as though he had two voices in his mind, and he was hearing first one, and then the other when he saw Elizabeth's rabbit nibbling some blades of grass. He grinned. "There's Bunny."

His boss, writing on a pad on his knee, looked up, "He has a hutch out here. Speaking of pets, how's our cat? Caught any mice lately?"

"It's still only a kitten," Kevin said quickly, then added, "I change the dirt in the box every day."

"I'm glad to hear it."

"There's a dog," Kevin said. A moment later, still looking out the window, "It came from the stables." And then, with alarm, "It's going after the rabbit." Without thinking, he pushed the window up, jumped out onto the iron balcony, and then leaped to the ground. Just in time. The dog, which was large and ferocious-looking, lunged at Bunny, who was backed into a corner by the wall.

Kevin jumped in front of the dog and felt the dog's teeth graze his wrist.

"You shouldn't have done that," a voice said from above him.

Kevin looked up and saw Christopher sitting on the wall dividing the garden from the one next door.

"She's your sister's rabbit," Kevin protested. "The dog would have killed it!"

"No, he wouldn't," Christopher said coldly. "He'd have stopped the minute my friend whistled. He's training him. But now you've spoiled it!"

At that moment Elizabeth burst through the back door. "Bunny!" she yelled. "Bunny!" She looked up at her brother. "What is Thor doing here, Chris?"

"I'm helping John train him," Christopher said in a long-suffering voice. At that point another boy pulled himself up on the wall between the gardens. "Where's Thor?"

"He was hunting the rabbit, as he was told to do, until he was stopped!" Christopher said.

"Who stopped him?"

Chris pointed at Kevin. "He did."

"Is he a friend of yours?" John asked. "He isn't from around here, is he?"

"No, he isn't," Christopher said. "He only works for my father—he's only a messenger!"

The other boy grinned. "Bite him, Thor! He doesn't belong here."

Thor, a big dog with a thick coat, growled and poised himself to lunge, whether toward Bunny or himself Kevin couldn't be sure.

"Stop that dog at once!" Mr. Langley's voice came from the window.

"But Papa—"

"At once, do you hear me, Christopher?"

"Stay, Thor!" The other boy's voice sounded deliberately resigned. The dog sat back.

"Christopher, Kevin, I want you both in my study. Now!"

When Kevin returned, he found his boss easing himself back onto his couch. He and Christopher stood for a moment staring at each other.

Mr. Langley looked at his son. "As I've explained, Christopher, I asked Kevin to come here to bring me work from the paper and take it back."

"Then what was he doing in our garden?"

Kevin burst out, "That dog was going to attack Bunny!"

"He'd have been stopped in time, if *you* hadn't interfered."

"Like this?" And Kevin held out his bleeding wrist.

Mr. Langley said angrily to his son, "You were using your sister's pet in some sort of game with a savage dog? It could have been killed."

"He'd have stopped, Papa—" Christopher started when Elizabeth darted in.

"Bunny could be dead!" she shouted at her brother.

"Of course he wouldn't! John's training Thor and he'd have stopped him—"

Mr. Langley spoke sharply. "If I *ever* hear of that happening again, Christopher, you will be punished severely. Do you understand me?"

Christopher swallowed. His face, which had gone red, was now white. He glanced at Kevin and then away. "Yes, Papa. But—"

"No buts, Christopher, that dog is not to come into our garden—ever!"

"But John's my best friend. We're in the same form in St. Andrew's. I told him I'd help in Thor's training."

"No!" Elizabeth cried. "He'll kill Bunny."

"Then why don't you keep her in the house? She's only a rabbit!"

"That's enough." Mr. Langley stared at his son. "Thor is not to come into our garden ever—under any circumstances. Is that clear?"

There was a silence. Then Christopher muttered, "Yes, Papa." Without looking at Kevin, he left.

"I'm sorry that happened, Kevin," Mr. Langley spoke abruptly. "Come over here." When Kevin walked over to the sofa, Mr. Langley said, "Stick out your wrist."

"It's not that—"

"Please do as I say."

Kevin held out his wrist. The bleeding had mostly stopped, and it was obvious the cuts were not deep.

"I hope to God that dog's mouth wasn't infected," Mr. Langley said, more or less to himself. "Elizabeth, go and get Bridie to bring some disinfectant and some cotton and a bandage."

"It's all right," Kevin muttered.

"Go on, Elizabeth."

"Yes, Daddy." She smiled at Kevin as she passed. "Bunny and I thank you."

When they'd come back, Langley himself doused the cotton with alcohol, dabbed it on Kevin's wrist, then wrapped the bandage around it. "That ought to hold it for the time being. I'm terribly sorry it happened."

Kevin was embarrassed. Used to Langley's distant manner, he found himself disconcerted by his kindness. "It doesn't hurt."

"I hope it stays that way. This material is ready now. You can take it back. I'll expect you tomorrow at the same time."

Kevin, pausing between chores at the paper, was reading that day's Letters column, when he suddenly burst out, "This letter says that councilman was right to call the Irish layabouts!"

Roberts looked over at him. "Well, he's entitled to say what he thinks." He saw Kevin staring at him. "Haven't you ever heard of the First Amendment?"

"First what?"

Roberts sighed. "Don't they teach you anything in school these days?" He smiled a little. "Or do you just not go very often? I'm talking about the First Amendment to the Constitution of the United States, which guarantees everybody the right to freedom of speech."

"'Course!" Kevin lied. "They talked about it in school only yesterday." He'd been too busy picking up extra pennies the previous day to go to school. "So if I write a letter saying it's a rotten lie you'll put it in the paper?"

Roberts laughed. "If that's all you have to say, I doubt it. It's too easy. You'd have to explain why you think it's a lie." As Kevin stared back at him, Roberts laughed. "I mean something besides loyalty."

"I know lots of Irish—me da's one—who work hard every day for next to nothing a week just to bring home food! Who's building the bridges and roads do you think!"

"Then say so. By the way, how *is* your father? The boss told me a while ago he'd had an accident."

"He's better. Maureen—me sister—and me are going to see him later this afternoon." He glanced at Maurice. "After I've taken the stuff up to Washington Square."

"Maureen and I," Roberts corrected automatically.

Kevin didn't say anything. He didn't like to be corrected—even by Roberts, whom he liked. But as he sat there, watching Roberts clattering away at his type-writer, he suddenly thought how wonderful it would be if he could do that, if he could be a top reporter. Then the other side, the side that spoke in Da's voice, told him not to be daft. Who'd hire a boy from the streets to be a writer? And he could imagine what jeers he'd get from the kids at school and the Mulberry Street gang if they knew he was even thinking of it. He pushed the idea away. But somehow Roberts's corrections didn't seem so bad.

He was walking by the northeast corner of the square when he saw Christopher standing about twenty feet away with some other boys. Christopher nudged one of the boys, pointed to Kevin, and they all laughed.

Kevin kept on walking. What he wanted to do was go over and punch Christopher. But there were five of them and one of him. And Christopher's father was his employer. Besides, he loved being on the paper. He walked steadily to the house, keeping his eyes so rigidly ahead that he almost walked into Elizabeth, who was playing with a ball in front of the house.

"Sorry," he muttered.

Elizabeth burst out, "I saw what happened, Kevin. Chris is a beast!"

Kevin looked at her. "I don't care," he said.

"Don't you? I know he's my brother, but I hate it when he acts that way. It's just to win favor with the boys at St. Andrews and the other Knickerbocker kids."

"I know some boys—the Mulberry Street Boys— that'd teach them a lesson pretty fast."

"But then there'd be a fight, Kevin, and that would upset Papa."

Kevin sighed. "I know."

Mr. Langley was writing when Kevin walked in. He looked up. "You're a little later than usual. Anything happen? At the paper, I mean?"

"No, sir," Kevin said. He approached the couch. "Jim sent these pieces about the plans for a big new building and wanted to know if you want a picture on the page."

"There can't be a picture, Kevin, if it hasn't been built yet!"

"I meant a drawing—I think Jim said it was a drawing—of the design for some steps."

"All right. Let me see." As Kevin handed over the drawing and an article, Langley handed him a copy of the paper. "I trust you've seen today's edition, Kevin."

"Yes, sir." While his boss was looking through the papers Jim had sent, he suddenly remembered the letter. "Roberts said I should write a letter to the paper answering the one this morning about Councilman Brown."

Langley, who was examining another article, said vaguely, "I suppose you're talking about Bill Reid's letter."

"What Councilman Brown said about the Irish being layabouts is a lie," Kevin said indignantly. "This man—" Kevin pointed to the letter in the paper "—says it isn't. But it is!"

Langley looked up at Kevin. "Roberts is right. If you feel that strongly about it, why don't you write a letter?"

"Will you tell Jim to put it in the paper?" Kevin still couldn't believe it.

"If it presents a valid point of view, we'll publish it." Langley looked at him. "Here's a pencil and some paper. You can use that desk over there."

"Now, sir?"

"Yes. Now. I want to see what you'd write."

For the next half hour Kevin toiled over the letter. Finally he finished and read it over.

His boss looked up. "Finished?"

Kevin nodded.

Langley held out his hand. "Let me have it."

Kevin brought over the single sheet of paper. Langley read aloud, "William Reid who says Councilman Brown is right about the Irish being layabouts is a bloody lair. It's plain he doesn't know anything about them!

"My father worked hard on the docks every day till he got hit by a load coming down off the ship. He's now in the hospital. He worked with lots of Irish, and they all work hard. They are on the job by seven in the morning and don't stop till six. I bet that's a lot harder than Councilman Brown works, or William Reid. I've been told Mr. Reid has the right to say what he wants because of the First Ammendment to the Constitution and the right of free speech, which says everybody can say what they want. But I think he's wrong, and I think somebody should say so. So I am now."

"Is it all right?" Kevin asked.

Langley looked up at him. "Yes. If you'll make some changes."

"What?" Kevin was gratified but suspicious.

"Take out 'bloody.' This is a family paper and it's considered a swear word."

"All right."

"And 'liar,' if you meant what I think you meant, is spelled i-a, not a-i. And amendment is spelled this way."

"Oh." Kevin took the sheet of paper.

"Here," Langley said, and handed him a pen. "And put in commas after 'William Reid' and 'layabouts.'"

"The teacher talks about commas. I can never see what they're for," Kevin grumbled.

"They make understanding the sentence easier. Read the sentence without stopping, and then read it, pausing at the commas. Go on, read it aloud."

Kevin did. Then he grinned.

"See what I mean?"

"Yes. That's funny."

"What's funny?"

"I thought you had to put in commas just because there were rules, and they'd mark you down if you didn't."

"If you're planning to have letters, or anything else, published, it's in your interest to make them as easy to read as possible." Langley paused. "That's what all newspapers are interested in. Getting the most readers." He smiled a little. "The more the better. And everybody has the right to say what *he* wants, not they."

"Oh." Kevin made the changes. Then he looked up. "Are you really going to run it?"

"Yes. Sign your name, and put your age beside it."

"Why?"

"Because I think it's important that anyone reading the letter knows that a boy who writes a letter can get it published in the paper. Not every twelve-year-old boy, of course. In fact, you may be the first in this city. You should be proud of yourself."

Kevin felt the blood rush into his face. Happy, but also embarrassed, he looked down.

"Put 'Kevin O'Donnell, aged twelve.'"

Kevin leaned over, signed the letter, and added "aged 12."

"Now take it back to Jim and tell him to run it as it is."

"Yes. Sir." He paused, aware suddenly that he wanted to say something, but didn't know how.

"Anything wrong?"

"No." Kevin looked down. Then, almost shyly, "Er—thanks."

Langley smiled a little. "You're welcome. By the way, I think you're going to make a good journalist—that is, *if* you stay in school!"

When Kevin got back to the paper he showed the letter to Roberts, who read it and said, "Take it over to Jim." Jim looked at it. Then he got up and went back over to Roberts. "The boss wants this printed as it is?"

"Yes. Exactly as it is."

"But—" Jim stopped.

"But what?"

"It could be better said."

"Not by a twelve-year-old boy. If you or I edited it, it would sound edited. This sounds real, exactly what a twelve-year-old boy might say." He grinned at Kevin. "Congratulations!"

Kevin, who was unused to praise, went red again.

Later that afternoon, Kevin said to Roberts, "I have to go by and get Maureen. We're going to the hospital to see Da."

"All right. Hope you find him better."

Kevin picked up Maureen at Mulberry Street, where she was playing skip rope with Eileen and Mary. "We have to get going to the hospital," he said.

They started the long walk up to Bellevue Hospital. By the time they got there, it was dark.

They found Frank O'Donnell in a long room with a lot of narrow beds. He was lying with his eyes closed, but when they walked up, he opened them.

"How are you, Da?" Maureen whispered. She leaned over and kissed his cheek. "We've been that worried about you!"

"The doctor says I can't go lifting any more heavy loads. I'll have to find another job."

"You'll get one, Da," Kevin said. He was standing on the other side of the bed. He thought his father's face was not as gray as it had been, but he was much thinner. "Are they feeding you right?" Kevin asked.

"Ay. But I'm not that hungry."

"Where's the doctor?"

"Somewhere around. They go in and out, like the nurses." He took a few breaths, which didn't sound quite as noisy as the ones when Kevin was visiting him before. Then, "There's one nurse who's very nice, Maggie Faolin from Clare. When she comes and feeds me, I eat more."

Maureen looked around. "Is she here, Da, now?"

"I don't know, Maureen. Like I said, they run here and there so fast. They're that busy."

"When do you think you'll be coming home?"

"The doctor hasn't said." He paused. "Has Timmins come back?"

"He's said he's coming back before the end of the month," Maureen said. "But he didn't say when."

"Just don't let him in," Frank said. He stirred restlessly. "If I could just be there—"

"Hello, Mr. O'Donnell. Are these your children?"

They looked up. A sturdy-looking young woman with a pleasant, freckled face was standing at the foot of the bed.

"This is Nurse Faolin," Frank said. And then, a little fretfully. "When do you think I'll be getting out of here, Nurse? The landlord could be coming by for the rent and with just these two there—"

"It'll be all right, Mr. O'Donnell. I'll have a word with the hospital. You mustn't let yourself worry. It'll just make things worse."

"How can I not worry? What would happen if my children were put out?" He started to try and get up.

"Now I want you to rest. And it's time for your medicine." She turned and looked at Kevin and Maureen. "Just step down to the end of the room and wait for me there, will you? I'll want to speak to the doctor and then have a word with you."

"Bye, Da," Maureen kissed her father again.

Kevin also kissed his father and squeezed his hand.

"Now just go down there and wait by the nurses' station," the young nurse said.

"He mustn't worry," Maureen said, as they walked to the end of the ward.

"No," Kevin agreed. But what would happen when Timmins came back?

In a few minutes the nurse joined them. "You must try not to worry him too much. It's not good for his heart."

"But he asked us questions," Maureen said.

"Do you want us to lie to him?" Kevin asked.

"It would be a good lie—at least for the time, until he's better," Nurse Faolin said. "Is there anywhere else you could get the money?"

They looked at each other. Finally Kevin said, "We'll find it."

♣ ♣ ♣

As they were leaving, they bumped into Father Martin of St. Catherine's church.

"Kevin, Maureen, what are you doing here? Have you been to see your father?"

"Yes, Father." Maureen added, "He was hurt bad."

"Sister Margaret told me he was." He eyed them. "How is he?"

"He's doing better," Kevin said.

"But he's not eating much," Maureen said sadly. "He's that thin."

"Umm. And how are the two of you doing?"

"It's—" Maureen started.

"We're doing fine, Father," Kevin interrupted, squeezing her hand. "Maureen's a grand cook."

Father Martin, a tall, dark-haired man in his forties, glanced at both of them. "I see," he said. "Well, your father was concerned about you when I saw him yesterday. He was worried about your rent and the landlord—what's his name?—"

"Timmins," Maureen said, ignoring Kevin, who was squeezing her hand again.

The priest looked at them again. "Well, I'm on my way to see him now. Let me know how the two of you get on."

"Yes, Father," Maureen said.

Father Martin's dark eyes rested on Kevin. "Well, Kevin?" he said.

"Yes, Father," Kevin said obediently.

"You know, Kevin, you can't run the whole world by yourself, although from everything I hear, you try."

Embarrassed, Kevin looked down.

"And what's this I hear about your working at the *Chronicle*?"

"It's true, Father," Maureen said. "He works hard."

"They're going to publish my letter," Kevin said, trying not to sound too proud.

"Are they now? When?"

"Kevin, you didn't tell me," Maureen said. "That's grand. Wait till I tell Eileen and Mary!"

"Yes, indeed. Be sure and let us know when it comes out! What's it about?"

"I'm saying that that man who called Irish layabouts was lying."

Father Martin laughed. "Wonderful! And they're publishing it? Good for them! Now, if you have any problems with Timmins, I want to know. All right?"

"Yes, Father," Maureen and Kevin said together.

"Kevin," Maureen said when they'd left the priest, "why didn't you want me to tell him about Timmins? He could maybe help us."

"Oh well," he said. "I thought I'd . . . I'd see what we could do first."

"Ma always said you were as stubborn as a pig," Maureen said. She added, "And she's right."

As they walked back to the tenement, Kevin didn't tell her that if anything kept their father from coming home, Sister Margaret or Father Martin, or both, might try and get them into the orphanage on Randalls Island. And Kevin didn't like that any better than being put out on the street—at least not for himself. How could he work on the paper if that happened?

Kevin stayed out of school the next day and looked for more jobs in various saloons. By noon he'd managed to pick up two pennies. Staring at them disgustedly, he suddenly remembered the dime the tailor on Hester Street had given him and walked quickly over there.

Going into the shop he asked, "Got any more letters to deliver?"

The man stared at him. Finally he said, "What's your name?"

"Kevin. Kevin O'Donnell."

After another minute, the man brought out another letter. "This is going to a man on Essex Street."

"Will you give me another dime?" Kevin asked.

"First deliver it—safely—and bring what I've asked for back here."

"What's he supposed to give me?"

"Three yards of cloth—for a suit I'm to make. And try not to get into a fight."

Kevin ran a few blocks over to Essex Street. He suddenly realized that the tailor had forgotten to tell him the name of the man on Essex. But although he couldn't read the name on the letter, he could read the address.

He walked slowly until the number over one of the narrow doors matched what was written on the letter.

The shop was down some steps and crowded with bolts of cloth.

Kevin ran down and peered in the door. Nobody seemed to be there. Squeezing in between the rolls of cloth, he finally saw a man, also wearing the same cap that the tailor on Hester Street wore, writing in the light of a kerosene lamp.

"Here's a letter for you," he said, holding it out.

The man looked up, stared at him for a minute, then took the letter and read it. Slowly he got up from his seat, went over, picked out one of the bolts of cloth and measured out three yards. After he'd cut the right amount, he folded it up, wrapped it in some newspaper, and handed it to Kevin. Kevin took the bundle. He'd been hoping this man would pay him, too. The man's large black eyes looked back at him. Then the man made a gesture, indicating Kevin was to go.

Kevin ran back to Hester Street and gave the cloth to the tailor there. The tailor put a nickel in his hand.

"I thought you were going to give me a dime."

"I gave you a dime last time because you got beaten up. But I'd only promised you a nickel. That's what

I'll give for taking a letter. Do you want the nickel or not?"

Kevin shrugged. "Yes." And then, "Thanks."

But as he made his way to the office all he could think about was how far he still was from having the rent money.

As the days passed, Kevin spent more and more time at Washington Square. Mr. Langley could walk now with the aid of a cane. But he still wasn't up to climbing the steep stairs at Park Row.

"There are stairs here, sir," Kevin said.

"Yes. But they're not as steep and there's always somebody here to help me. Anyway, I'm going to operate here for a while longer, Kevin. And I'm afraid this means you'll be running back and forth a lot, but it can't be helped."

And then one day Kevin found himself writing at his boss's dictation. "I can't write that fast," Kevin protested as the words came fast and faster.

"All right, but write as fast as you can. This has to get written and downtown for tomorrow's paper." Mr. Langley obediently slowed for a few sentences, but inevitably the words started coming more quickly again. Finally, in desperation, Kevin invented his own shorthand.

When he'd finished, the boss held out his hand. "Let me look at it."

"Well, I—"

"Come on now!"

"I didn't write out all the words, sir."

"I daresay I'll be able to make it out. I pretty much remember what I said." When Kevin brought over the paper he looked at it. "What on earth?" he started. Then, "Oh . . . I see." After perusing it he said, "Not bad. Now write it out properly."

When Kevin had finished, he read it through again. "Yes," he said when he'd finished. "You seem to have gotten it down pretty well. But—" He looked up at Kevin. "Don't they teach you spelling at school?"

Kevin felt his cheeks get hot. "'Course they do. Only—"

"Only you don't pay much attention, or—" One brow went up. "Or have you been missing school lately?"

In an effort to earn whatever he could, Kevin had been missing school more and more frequently while he looked for odd jobs in the morning. But knowing the boss wanted—and expected—him to attend school, he was afraid to admit any of this. So he stared down at his shoes.

"All right, Kevin, I'm going to write out the correct spelling of every word I've marked. I want you to write them after me and learn them by heart. I don't want to see these words misspelled again. All right? And I expect you to go to school. That's part of our agreement!"

Kevin grunted. Then said, "Yes, sir."

"Did I give you the editorial?"

"Yes, sir. But—" He stopped.

"But what?"

"Yesterday you said you were going to write one about landlords being unfair to tenants. But you wrote about Garfield's new administration."

"And you think the way landlords treat their tenants is more important?"

"Yes. Timmins—our landlord—is always trying to turn people out."

Mr. Langley eyed him. "You speak with some feeling. Is that what your landlord is doing now?"

"Yes. It's not just me that's saying so."

"It's not just I," Mr. Langley corrected. "Who else?"

"Everybody in the house. Mrs. Barnes was turned out last month and all her stuff thrown into the street. Without any notice. Also the Flahertys, right after he lost his job. Timmins didn't even give him a chance to find a new one. And he raises the rent all the time."

"That's outrageous!" Mr. Langley said. "We must certainly add an editorial about that." He looked up at Kevin. "By the way, how is your father? Still in the hospital?"

"Yes." Kevin burst out, "He looks that thin! He doesn't eat enough. He was asking us about the landlord, but the nurse stopped us from talking. She said he was not to be worried."

Mr. Langley was watching him. "She's probably right. Why don't you begin the editorial about how the landlords treat tenants—at least the opening? I can take it from there."

Kevin, both flattered and nervous, pulled over a sheet of paper. After a minute of thinking he wrote, "Landlords are cruel to threaten people and their children, saying they'll be thrown out just because they're a bit behind in their rent. Everybody is some of the time. And then the poor people and their children have nowhere to go but the streets!"

Mr. Langley had been watching him. "All right. Let me see."

Kevin got up and took his sheet of paper over.

"Not bad," Langley said. He made a few corrections and handed the sheet back.

Kevin read: "Landlords have no right to evict tenants and their families without warning simply because they are temporarily behind in their rent. It is cruel and inhuman!"

"Yes," Kevin said. "That's good." He then added, curious, "Where d'you learn grammar like that?"

"Going to school and working on the paper." Langley looked up. "As you do."

"Yes," Kevin said. "I do." He told himself it was mostly the truth.

"Good. Now add this," and Langley dictated: "There is a growing movement in the legislature to establish a commission to investigate and inquire into the condition of tenement houses, lodging houses, and cellars in the city. The abuses by landlords are becoming a disgrace." He looked at Kevin. "That should do it."

Elizabeth, who had come in quietly and been sitting in the corner reading, put her hand up in front of her face and giggled.

Her father smiled a little. "There you are, Lizzie. What's so funny?"

"I hate that name," Elizabeth said.

He sighed. "My apologies. Elizabeth."

"You sound just like a teacher."

"Is that bad?"

"Well . . . " Elizabeth grinned at Kevin, who grinned back.

That was also the day Kevin discovered another aspect of life in Washington Square.

As soon as Elizabeth had left, Kevin said, "Excuse me, sir, but where's the privy?" He knew there had to be one, but he hadn't seen it when he was in the garden. This was such a grand place it was probably hidden somewhere.

Langley looked up. "There's a toilet on the floor above and another one next to the kitchen on the floor below. Why don't you go to the one upstairs?"

Except for the tiny room containing a water closet at the *Chronicle,* Kevin had never seen an inside bathroom and was pretty sure no one he knew had, either. He stood up. "All right, sir."

He went upstairs. When he reached the top he looked at the various doors facing the staircase. One was ajar, and he saw the edge of something resembling an oversized sink, so he went in there.

It was a revelation. For fifteen minutes Kevin happily turned the water on and off, smoothed his hand over the immaculate white porcelain, and stared in wonder and admiration at the deep, enormous bathtub, imagining how wonderful it would be to lie in there covered by water. As he did, he thought about the privy at the back of the tenement on Mulberry Street, the overflowing chamber pots that had to be carried down the flights of stairs, or sometimes emptied out the windows, and the stench that never seemed to go away. . . .

Kevin left the bathroom and started down the stairs. He was halfway down when he saw Christopher come through the front door.

"What are you doing up there?" Christopher demanded. "You have no right to go into the rest of the house."

"Your da told me to use the toilet there," Kevin replied indignantly.

"My papa would never allow someone like you to go to that part of the house. Papa!" he called, going toward the back room.

Kevin ran down. As he approached, he heard his boss say, "I did tell Kevin he could use either the toilet downstairs, or the one upstairs. Why are you making a fuss about it?"

At that moment, Mrs. Langley entered. "What's going on? Christopher?"

Her son turned, "Papa's messenger boy was upstairs using our bathroom. And we don't know where else he was poking about up there."

"I wasn't poking about anywhere," Kevin said.

"Christopher, for heaven's sake, will you come off this ludicrous upper-class act?" Mr. Langley said. "This is the United States, the country, in case you haven't heard, where all men, regardless of poverty or circumstance, are supposedly created equal."

"Yes, but—"

"As I've told you before, Kevin is my employee. He's here at my request to help me out while I cope with this leg. And I insist that you apologize to him now for your rudeness—"

"Really, James, is this necessary?" Mrs. Langley said.

"Yes." Mr. Langley kept his eyes on Christopher. "For your rudeness, which is unacceptable." As his son continued to stare at him, he said, "Well?"

"James, can't we—"

"After Christopher has apologized to Kevin."

For a moment, Kevin's eyes rested on Elizabeth, who was still sitting in a little chair in a corner of her father's room. Her eyes, wide and gray, were on her brother.

There was a moment's silence. Then Christopher said between narrowed lips, "Sorry."

"Not to me," Mr. Langley said. "To Kevin."

Christopher turned slightly toward Kevin, but still didn't look him in the eye. "Sorry," he muttered, staring past Kevin's shoulder, then he ran out and upstairs.

"I really do think—" Mrs. Langley started.

"Just a moment, my dear," Mr. Langley said. "Kevin, I want you to get these down to the paper as fast as you can. I'll talk to Jim on the phone about exactly what I want done, but to get in tomorrow's edition these have got to be there immediately." He swept up the papers and held them out to Kevin. "Now get going!"

"Yes, sir," Kevin said. He picked up his bag from the chair, pushed the papers inside, and headed for the front door. But as he was closing the front door behind him, he heard Mrs. Langley, her voice lowered, talking to her husband, "I really do think, James, to embarrass Christopher before your messenger, however highly you may think of him, is very wrong. Christopher's only reflecting the principles on which he has been brought up—"

"Your principles, my dear," Kevin heard Mr. Langley say clearly. "I've never taught him to talk down to other people."

"I suppose that means you think I have."

There was a silent pause. Kevin started to ease the front door shut, when he heard Mr. Langley say, "Not so much you, but your family and that snobbish school he goes to."

"Would you rather he went to the public school, like your messenger?"

"It wouldn't hurt him, my dear."

"Perhaps you think it wouldn't. But I'm afraid I can't agree with you. Some of the children who are there come from families that are dirty and illiterate."

Kevin heard Langley clear his throat. Then he said, "Perhaps if your forebears had suffered through the famine and been turned off their farms, they'd be dirty and illiterate, too."

There was another pause.

"I see your point, James. But you don't help your son by embarrassing him in front of . . . of your messenger. And you don't help your messenger, either."

"His name is Kevin, Emily."

"I sometimes think you like him a great deal more than you like your own son."

"Don't be ridiculous! I admire him, because in spite of all his disadvantages, he's bright, hardworking, and helps support a sister, now that his father is in the hospital. He doesn't have an easy time."

There was another pause. Then Mrs. Langley said, "Although you probably won't believe me, neither does Christopher." She paused. "Well, I'll leave you now. Come, Elizabeth."

"But I want to stay in here, Mama."

"No, Elizabeth, I want you with me."

Kevin closed the door as quietly as possible, then ran down the steps, and across the square.

As he first walked and then ran downtown, Kevin's mind savored the huge—and astonishing—satisfaction of having Christopher apologize to him, obviously hating every minute of it. He grinned at the gratifying memory of the boy's pained face. Then he went back over that fragment of conversation he'd overheard between the boss and his wife.

It had never occurred to him that Mr. Langley, the owner of the paper, actually liked him, let alone respected him. The more he thought about it, the more confused he felt, oddly happy one minute, disturbed the next, almost as though he wanted to cry, which upset him. Men didn't cry, and he was a man. Or almost. It was years since he'd felt like that, and he found it discomfiting, almost embarrassing. So he pushed it all to the back of his mind as he ran. Then he found himself thinking about Da and the things he'd said about the rich and the mighty and how they'd get everything out of you, then cheat you if they could. But it wasn't true of Mr. Langley.

· "Don't be daft," his father's voice echoed in Kevin's mind. "Of course it's true. He wants something out of you. . . . " The argument went back and forth in Kevin's mind. Sometimes he saw and heard his father. Sometimes it was Mr. Langley's face and voice. He shook his head as he came to the corner and waited for the carriages to pass.

He finally got to the paper and emptied the contents out on Jim's desk. Jim sifted through the papers. "The boss sure isn't taking time off, is he?" he said. He pulled out a sheet of paper and read it. "Did you write this?"

"Yes, sir. . . . " then added, "Mr. Langley dictated it."

"And he seems to have corrected your spelling."

"Yes, sir."

"All right. I've got some more stuff for you to deliver." Jim glanced over a pile of pictures. "That lot needs to go back now. I guess that's all for today. Tomorrow's Saturday. No school. So be here at eight."

Kevin was opening the door, when Jim said suddenly, "By the way, we're running your letter tomorrow."

Kevin stared. "Tomorrow?"

"That's right. Tomorrow. That's what the boss said he wanted."

Kevin grinned delightedly, then left.

After he'd delivered the pictures, it was dusk. Kevin stood for a moment on the sidewalk. What he ought to do was go and see if he could pick up any work in the theaters that would be opening by now.

But he didn't move. Instead he found himself thinking again about the conversation between Mr. and Mrs. Langley that he'd overheard, about Christopher apologizing to him, and his letter appearing in the paper tomorrow. It was all so unbelievable. He felt an overwhelming need to tell somebody.

Quickly he went down to Mulberry Street and ran up the stairs. But Maureen wasn't there. Neither, of course, was Da. As he stood at the door, Mrs. Lafferty looked in from across the tiny hall. "Maureen told me to tell you she's gone to St. Patrick's with her class for a special celebration of some kind."

For a minute Kevin stood there, feeling let down. Then he ran down the stairs again with the intention of locating Tommy Meehan. But the more he thought about it, the less sure he was that telling Tommy and the other Mulberry Street Boys was a good idea. He stood on the street outside the house and then decided to go to the hospital to see his father.

Frank O'Donnell looked better than he had a few days before, less pale and more alert.

"How are you, Da?" Kevin asked.

"Better, Kev. Thanks to Nurse Faolin. She's been grand." He paused and tried pulling himself up a little. "Give us a hand, Kev."

Kevin leaned over his father, trying to pull him up by the shoulders.

"Careful there," Nurse Faolin came around the other side. "Let's go easy now."

Gently they pulled Frank O'Donnell up.

"You look better, Da," Kevin said.

"I'm feeling better, Kevin." He looked up at the nurse, with her curly brown hair showing under her cap, "and it's all due to Nurse Faolin here."

The nurse smiled a little. Her cheeks were pink. "Now don't be forgetting the doctors, Mr. O'Donnell, and the good Lord Himself. I always say rosaries for my patients."

"You've been grand to me!" Kevin saw his father reach up and clasp the nurse's hand.

She blushed more. "Go on!" She glanced over at Kevin.

"I'll be going now to see to my other patients." She smiled at Kevin. "Now, don't be telling your father anything that's going to upset him."

"I won't," Kevin said.

"Come on, lad," Frank said when the nurse's back receded down the narrow space between the rows of beds. "Tell me about you and Maureen. Has Timmins come back?"

"No, Da. He hasn't."

"Don't answer the door if he does. I'll be out of here soon and I'll find the money somehow."

Kevin saw that his father looked less cheerful than he had a minute or two before. "Da, my letter's going to be in the paper tomorrow."

"What letter, Kev?"

"The one I wrote saying Irish aren't layabouts, that Councilman Brown was wrong when he said that, and I wrote about how hard you and other Irish workers work. The boss said I was to write the letter and Jim said it was going to run tomorrow!"

"I'll believe that when I see it," Frank said.

"But, Da, he told me. And Mr. Langley also said I was smart and worked hard and would be a good journalist. And he made Christopher apologize when he was rude. And today he let me write a short editorial about how mean landlords are." It all tumbled out. But his father's response was not what he'd hoped for.

"Now you listen to me, Kevin. I've told you before, you can't go trusting these bosses. The next thing you know your job will be given to some friend of his son's, some kid from a rich school."

"But, Da—"

"You listen to what I say! And now you can help me lie down again. I'm not feeling that strong. Is a nurse around anywhere?"

Kevin tried to ease his father down into the narrow bed and looked around to see if Nurse Faolin was anywhere. But she seemed to be out of the ward for the moment.

"You can go now, Kev. I'm tired and I think I'll just rest."

Kevin left the hospital. The visit hadn't gone the way he'd planned at all. What Da had said about Mr. Langley and his motives upset him. And his reminder of Timmins also disturbed him. Somewhere, somehow, he'd have to find some money.

The next morning Kevin showed up at the paper a little before eight, excited about seeing his letter in the paper. He was also carrying some milk for the kitten who was waiting for him inside the door, meowing loudly. He was now older and leggy and always hungry.

When Kevin opened the door, Mickey, as he'd come to call the cat, laid the remains of a mouse at Kevin's feet.

"Hey, look, he's killed a mouse!" Kevin shouted. He felt proud.

Jim glanced over. "It's about time. He's got to earn his wage like everybody else. And by the way, his box needs changing. I can smell it from here!"

"Change it now, Kevin," Roberts said. "Before you do anything else. I beg you!"

"I want to see my letter first!" Kevin said, grabbing the paper off Roberts's desk.

"It's not there," Roberts said quickly. And then, "I'm sorry, but the boss telephoned and said he wanted us to put in a letter from a reader concerning our story about John Kelly and the Tammany factions. And he said he thought your letter would carry more weight in a Sunday edition, anyway. Don't look like that, Kevin, he's right. Plenty of people buy and read the Sunday papers who don't bother with the daily. They figure whatever's important will be there Sunday."

"Yeah," Kevin said. He knew what Roberts said was true. But his father's embittered warning loomed large. He pushed it back and, after he'd changed the cat's dirt, went off to pick up a story that the City Hall reporter had scribbled, before he went off for another story in Brooklyn. At three, Jim said, "The boss wants you up in Washington Square."

For the next several days, Kevin was kept busy dashing between Park Row and Washington Square, taking papers back and forth, sometimes several times a day. Often he passed Christopher, either in the square or in the house. Christopher always pretended not to see him, so Kevin did the same.

One Saturday when Kevin rang and was let into the house by Bridie, he saw a purse lying on the hall table. He opened his mouth to say something, then didn't, afraid it would sound stupid. After all, it wasn't his house. So why shouldn't Mrs. Langley, or Elizabeth, leave a purse lying on the hall table? Except that it looked strange in a household where nothing ever seemed out of place. And it didn't look like anything Elizabeth or a girl would carry. So it must be Mrs. Langley.

"Your ma left a purse on the table in the hall," Kevin said to Elizabeth, who was sitting in the corner of her father's room reading.

"Yes. She sometimes leaves it there. She says it's so she won't have to go looking for it."

Mr. Langley shuffled the papers in his hand. "Polish up your shorthand, Kevin. I want to dictate an editorial for tomorrow's paper. All right? Are you ready?"

"Yes, sir."

When Langley finished and Kevin, more adept at taking dictation now than he had been, had read it back so Mr. Langley knew he had put it down correctly, his boss said, "I want you to get that down to the paper now. If there's anything else, I'll hold it for when you come back."

As he was leaving, Kevin said, "My letter wasn't in the paper on Tuesday."

"No, Kevin. It's going in on Sunday. I'm sorry about not putting it in Tuesday, but more people will see it on Sunday. Didn't Roberts tell you that?"

"Yes, he did. Sir."

"It'll appear on Sunday. I promise. Now get that downtown and then come back."

Kevin barely paused when he got to the paper, handing the editorial to Jim, only to get another set of papers. "Sorry to send you back so fast. But I want the boss to see these as soon as possible. So get back up there now."

It was a hot day and by the time Kevin got back up to Washington Square he was sweating, and his clothes were sticking to him.

Kevin took off his jacket. His shirt wasn't clean, certainly not in comparison to the boss's, who'd also removed his jacket and had the window open. But he couldn't help it. Since Da was in the hospital no washing had been done.

Kevin looked around to see where he could put his jacket. "Where can I hang this, sir?" Kevin asked. Mr. Langley's jacket was draped over the only possible chair in the room, because the chair Elizabeth was sitting in was small, and her father's jacket would have dragged on the ground.

"You can put it on Elizabeth's chair," Mr. Langley said.

"It's too long for this chair," Elizabeth said. "It'll drag on the floor. I'll put it in the hall for him."

"All right, Elizabeth, take it out for him, would you? I want to get this dictated and back to Park Row."

Elizabeth left with the coat. Kevin sat down to take Mr. Langley's dictation. The boss dictated so quickly that Kevin hardly noticed how long Elizabeth was gone or when she came back, and was only vaguely aware of voices in the hall.

"All right," Mr. Langley said when Kevin had finished reading the article back to him. "Get that back downtown. I want it to be in the paper tomorrow."

Kevin went out into the hall, got his jacket, and returned to put the papers into the bag to take back to the paper. He was doing that when Christopher came in, followed by Elizabeth.

"Somebody's stolen some money from Mama's purse," Christopher said. He looked directly at Kevin. "Six dollars are gone."

"Maybe she forgot she'd spent it," Langley said, getting his papers together.

"No, she didn't, Papa. I asked her that."

At that moment Mrs. Langley appeared in the doorway. "I'm very sorry to have to say that someone has taken money from my purse." She'd been looking at Kevin, but her eyes shifted to her husband.

He straightened. "What are you suggesting, Emily?"

"I think, as the head of this household, you should investigate any thievery that goes on in your home. Six dollars may not seem like a great deal of money, but in certain quarters of this city it would seem so."

Kevin, standing there with the bag under his arm, stared at her.

"Are you suggesting that one of our servants took it?" Mr. Langley asked. He sounded astonished.

"No, not one of our servants," Mrs. Langley spoke slowly. Her voice was cold.

"It was him," Christopher said, pointing to Kevin.

Afterward Kevin was furious at himself for not seeing what was going on sooner, especially after all his father's warnings.

"I didn't steal the money!" Kevin yelled. "When would I have done that?"

"Oh, yes, you did!" Christopher darted forward. "I'm going to see what's in your jacket!" And before Kevin knew what was happening, Christopher was plunging his hand into Kevin's jacket.

"Stop that!" Mr. Langley said. "Stop that at once!"

"You look!" Christopher said.

"I certainly will not!" Mr. Langley said.

"Then you'll leave your own son looking a liar, and we will never know if your precious messenger is indeed innocent!" said Mrs. Langley.

Mr. Langley stared at his wife. Then he turned to Kevin. "Would you object to showing us what's in your pockets, Kevin?"

Kevin felt sick, humiliated, and furious at himself for ever believing in this man. "So *you* think I've stolen, too! Here—"

He rammed his hands into his pockets and pulled them out. Dollar bills scattered over the floor.

There was a moment's silence, while they all looked at the bills. Suddenly Elizabeth burst into tears.

"Perhaps, James, you will acknowledge now that Christopher was telling the truth," Mrs. Langley said.

Kevin raised his head and stared at Christopher. "You put this here. I didn't steal any money."

"I've been outside. Ask Elizabeth. We were in the garden. It was Mama who found it out when she was going shopping."

Mr. Langley looked at his wife and son, and then at his daughter. "Elizabeth?" he asked.

But Elizabeth, sobbing, ran out of the room.

"There are only five dollars on the floor," Mrs. Langley said. "Where is the sixth?"

Kevin put his hands in his pockets, found a dollar bill in one, and threw it on the floor with the others.

Mr. Langley looked at Kevin. "I wish you hadn't felt the need to do this, Kevin. I know times are hard and your father's in the hospital, but—"

"You think I stole the money, too, don't you?"

"The evidence is pretty strong."

"I never stole from you before. I told you about the extra dollar!"

"We met because you did. You stole copies of the paper. Have you forgotten?"

Kevin had. "That's different. It was only a paper!"

"Stealing is stealing," Mrs. Langley said.

A sense of betrayal beyond anything he had ever known swept through Kevin. This was the man who, unknown to Kevin himself, had become the father Da could never really be. At that moment he was terrified that he'd be sick or burst into tears. Either would be horrible and would humiliate him. He flung the bag at his boss's feet on the sofa. "You can keep your stinking job!"

He turned and ran out of the room and out of the house.

He had run out of the house, across the square, and past Broadway to the Bowery before he realized tears were on his cheeks.

"What's the matter, lad? Somebody take away your dollie?" a jeering voice said.

Kevin stopped. A man, holding a glass of beer, was standing outside one of the Bowery's many saloons, leaning against the door. There was a grin on his face.

Kevin stared at him, angry and embarrassed. Then he ran down the Bowery and veered off toward Mulberry. But what was the point of going home? Maureen would be in school and Da was still in Bellevue.

He stood there on the street, an empty feeling inside him. How long had he been at the paper? He tried to remember. In some ways it seemed as though he'd been there forever. What had he done before that? Gone to school, delivered messages, looked for work . . .

But Da was working then, bringing home his pay. It wasn't a lot, but it paid the rent. The rent . . . Timmins . . .

Kevin started walking.

"Hey, Kevin!"

Kevin turned.

"What you doing, Kev? Thought you had a job."

It was Tommy Meehan and some of the Mulberry Street Boys.

"A real fancy job on a newspaper," one of the Lafferty boys said. They were all leaning against the wall of a bar. "Maureen was telling me sister."

"What happened? Get fired? Get the can?" sneered a third boy.

"Come on, lads," Tommy said. "He's not doing anything wrong." He and the other boys started to walk away. But one turned back.

"Don't they want you anymore? Nick something?"

Kevin had landed his fist in the boy's nose before he knew what he was doing. The next thing he was aware of, he was lying on the ground, being kicked.

"Stop it!" Tommy shouted. "Come on now!"

But the boy who'd sneered at him was looking down on Kevin as he tried to get up. "That's for thinking you were better than us with your fancy job!"

"Are you all right?" Tommy asked.

Kevin sat up on the curb. "Yes. Just go away!"

"Are you sure?" Tommy asked anxiously.

"Yes! Just go!"

"All right. Come on, lads!" Tommy said, and they walked off.

Kevin's nose was still bleeding and he felt a little sick. So he sat on the curb holding his hands over his face. He could feel the blood still dripping through his fingers. But after a while it stopped.

"Good heavens, Kevin! What on earth happened to you?"

Kevin took his hands away from his face and looked up. It was Father Martin.

"Here, use this," Father Martin said, holding out a handkerchief.

Kevin took it and started wiping his face.

"No, that just smears it around." The priest looked up. "McLarney's Saloon. Umm. Well, at least they'll have some water in here. Come along!"

"I don't—" Kevin started.

"No, you're going to come in here with me. Come along now!"

"No—" Kevin started. He didn't want Father Martin to know what had happened to him. Father Martin was the kind of priest who always tried to get people out of trouble. But he'd probably bring up the subject of Kevin's being an altar boy again. And that meant he'd be able to keep a close eye on what Kevin did most of the time. Kevin would have to behave himself—no running messages from saloons or other places like that.

"I'll be all right," Kevin said, getting to his feet.

"You can't go around with blood all over your face, Kevin. Now come along."

The next thing Kevin knew they were in the saloon and Father Martin was asking for a glass of water.

The barman looked at Kevin. "You're in a real muck!" he said. Then he brought the glass of water. "Here!" He also brought out a bowl, which he filled from the sink underneath the bar. "And this." And he handed over a towel.

Father Martin went to work on Kevin's face. "There," he said after some vigorous scrubbing and wiping. "That's better. There's some on your shirt. You'll have to go home and put on another one." He lowered the rag. "Do you have a clean shirt?"

Kevin mumbled something. He hadn't washed any shirts lately, and he knew Maureen hadn't, either.

Father Martin handed the cloth back to the man behind the bar. "Thanks for the water." He put his hand on Kevin's shoulder. "Kevin, what are you going to do now? And why aren't you at your job?"

Kevin looked up into the kind but penetrating dark eyes. Then he looked quickly away, shame washing over him. "I have to go now, Father. I've a job I'm doing." And before Father Martin could say or do anything, Kevin was out the door and running down the street, as though the shame itself was pursuing him.

He ran as far and as long as he could. When he was finally out of breath, he stopped and looked around him and realized he was on lower Broadway where there were handsome shops and brownstones and the gas streetlights were coming on. It was too late to look for a daytime job. His only chance tonight would be back on the Bowery where he could maybe find a job running errands for one of the theaters or saloons. Maureen would be home by now. He'd better go back there.

Maureen was busy cooking some potatoes when he climbed the steps to their apartment.

"Where have you been, Kevin? You're late."

"Doing errands."

"What happened to you, Kev? Father Martin was here. He said you were being beat up. And your face is puffed up."

Kevin wished the good priest weren't quite as good. "I got in a bit of a fight with some of the Mulberry Street Boys."

"Oh, Kev! You know they're always in trouble. What were you fighting about?"

Kevin hesitated. He didn't want to mention his job—his former job.

"What, Kev?"

"Nothing much. They thought I was stuck-up."

"It's likely about your job. I told Sister Margaret about it. She was ever so pleased." There was a pause. Trying to avoid a painful admission, Kevin couldn't think of anything to say. But he knew he'd have to tell Maureen sooner or later about leaving his job.

"I left the job, Maureen."

"But you liked it so much, and you've been there so long. Why?" She paused. "Did they fire you?"

"No." He swallowed. "Christopher, the boss's son, said I'd stolen some money."

"Oh, Kev." She paused. "Did you?"

"You know I didn't. I'd not've stolen from the boss."

"Then why did he say you did?"

"Because he's a stuck-up prig and the boss made him apologize to me, and he was getting his own back." As Kevin said that, the whole thing was suddenly clear to him. He'd been too upset to see it before. "Him and his ma."

"How horrible! I thought you said they were nice!" She stared at her brother and then said slowly, "So you think Christopher made it look like you were stealing?"

"Well, I didn't steal, but when I said that to the boss he said I'd stolen the papers when we met and he offered me the job."

Maureen stared at her brother. "Did you, Kev?"

"Everybody steals papers, Maureen. They're only a penny."

"It's still wrong! You know that! Sister Margaret says—"

"Are you on their side now?" Kevin shouted.

"You know I'm not! I think what he did was horrible." She went over and put her hands on Kevin's shoulders. "Don't be cross, now!"

Kevin clamped his teeth together to keep from crying. "It's all right," he muttered.

"But what're we going to do? Mrs. Lafferty said Timmins was back. He said he was going to throw our things out and have us sent to Randalls Island."

"I'll think of something," Kevin muttered.

It was a dreadful week, beginning with seeing his letter in the *Chronicle*. He had thought, of course, they wouldn't run it after everything that had happened. But Sunday morning, after Mass, he had slid a *Chronicle* off the top of a pile in front of the newsstand near St. Catherine's Church. When he saw the owner looking at him, he put a penny on the counter and went on looking. When he saw his letter he gave a shout, and ran home to show Maureen.

Kevin spent the week looking for a job. He still had almost two dollars from his last pay. With it he bought a little bread, milk, and some cod. When he brought the milk home he remembered Mickey and worried about who would feed him. But he didn't mention it to Maureen, who would worry, too. He thought about trying to steal the cat back from the office when no one was there, but he knew Da would be home before long, and he'd put him out in no time. The boss had been kind about Mickey, but Kevin didn't want to think about the boss. It made him angry and it was painful, because every time he thought about the boss, he lived again through the terrible moment when the boss had accused him of stealing. So he said nothing and went on looking for a new job. He picked up an occasional nickel here and there. But he didn't find anything.

He knew he ought to go and see his father in Bellevue. But he also knew his father would have the details of what had happened at the *Chronicle* out of him in no time, so he postponed it each day.

Then one day Maureen told him she'd been to see Da on her way home from school and had told him what had happened. His father wanted him to visit him right away.

When Kevin went, it was exactly the way he'd imagined.

"I've told you, Kev, not to trust these high and mighties," his father said, when he turned up. "Your sister told me all about it, and I'm telling you this. If I wasn't here, flat in me bed, I'd go and give that man—what was his name did you tell me?—Langley, what I think of him. It's a disgrace. You'd not steal anything!"

"No, Pa. Well, I've taken a penny paper—"

"That's wrong and you're not to do it again, Kevin, do you hear me? But it's a far cry from stealing money, and when I get out of here, I'll be going up and telling that high-nosed man what I think of him. Just because he's got money—"

Kevin was torn. He was touched more than he wanted to admit at his father's loyalty. But somehow, thinking of his father in that office, or in the Washington

Square house, he seemed to Kevin frail, too easily subject to being hurt or wounded.

"Don't think about it now, Da."

"Don't you be telling me what I ought to think about, Kevin. I'll have you know, when I was younger and stronger—" As he went on, he tried to pull himself up in the bed. His face flushed and he seemed short of breath.

"Don't, Da, it's all right. Don't try and get up like that!"

"Now, Frank, you're not to push yourself. I've told you that before." Nurse Faolin hurried up. "Just you rest easy! It's not worth your getting yourself upset." She turned toward Kevin, who was standing on the other side of the bed. "Now is it?" she said severely.

"No, Da, I told you. I'll get another job."

"I'll tell that man what—"

"When you're better, Frank. When you're strong again and won't hurt yourself! D'ye hear me now? You'll not be helping Kevin by dropping dead, now will you?"

It was said in a joking voice, but Kevin knew she wasn't joking. She turned to Kevin. "Tell him, Kevin, tell him you're going to be fine. You're a big lad now, you'll be getting another job soon now, won't you?"

"Ay, Da. I'll be working another job before you know it."

"And what about school, Kev? You'll not be getting anywhere without some learning. I was talking to

Father Martin about it, when he came to see me. He said you're to go talk to him. Now, listen, Kevin, I want you to promise me you'll do that. Talk to the good father. Promise!"

"Da, of course I will. I promise!"

Some of the dangerous color went out of his father's cheeks. "You do that. We all have to stick together, Kev. Now promise!"

"Da, I promise."

"I'll be out of here soon." He looked up at the nurse. "And Nurse Faolin has said she'd be kind enough to look in on us at home, haven't you, m'dear?"

Her cheerful, freckled face broke into a grin. "I have, Frank."

He glanced over at Kevin. "Has Timmins been back?"

"He—" Kevin started. He didn't want to lie again, but he also knew now his father mustn't be excited. "No, Da, he hasn't."

His father stared at him. "Are you lying to me, Kev?"

"No, Da."

"And now you're going to lie back down again and have a wee nap, Frank. I'll be getting your medicine. Now say good-bye, Kevin, I know you have to go."

"Ay, I do. I'll be back . . . tomorrow."

He didn't want to return so soon. He wanted to spend the time looking for a job, but he thought it might soothe his father a little to say he'd be back.

"All right," his father said tiredly. "But watch your-self. There's some kind of parade tomorrow. I heard the other patients talking about it. Remember last year when there was a parade? I was at work so you picked up Maureen at school." His father paused for a few labored breaths. "She has to cross Broadway, Kev, to get home. I don't want her doing that alone. It wouldn't be safe."

"Of course he'll pick her up, won't you, Kevin?" Nurse Faolin said. "So you don't have anything to worry about." She turned to Kevin and said cheerfully. "Now, Kevin, tell your father you'll do as he asks. Then he's got to get some rest!" The nurse, though smiling, was telling Kevin what to do. "I'll see you at the door of the ward," she said firmly.

"Bye, Da," Kevin said, and went down to the end of the ward.

When Nurse Faolin came up she pulled him out into the little hall and said, "Don't be disturbing your da, now."

"I thought he was a lot better."

"He is, if he isn't worried or riled up. So be a good boy now, and just you remember that!"

He'd have to get back and remind Maureen that tomorrow he'd pick her up at school.

The next morning Kevin skipped school and spent an hour looking for odd jobs. By the time he picked up Maureen at St. Catherine's he still hadn't earned anything and he was ravenously hungry. When he got to the school, he found a lot of the children in the yard.

Maureen was excited. "We were let out early because of the parade."

"I'm taking you home," Kevin said.

"But Eileen and I want to watch the parade. It ought to be fun."

"Maureen, there could be trouble. Remember Joe Williams from Sullivan Street? He got into a terrible fight two years ago at some parade."

"But he was a bully, Kevin. The police arrested him."

"Maybe. Come on, Maureen, let's go."

"Can't we wait for Eileen? She'll be out in a minute. Please!"

"No, Maureen. I've got to find another job afterward."
He took her hand and pulled her away.

"Kevin!" Maureen said later, as they walked quickly
uptown. Maureen was panting a little because Kevin,
who was much taller and had longer legs, was setting a
fast pace.

"What?"

"You're walking too fast for me. I'm puffed."

He looked at her. "All right," he said, and started
walking more slowly.

The parade was two or three blocks away, coming
up Broadway, just as Kevin and Maureen got there.
Maureen forgot she was mad and jumped up and down
with excitement.

They were standing there, watching, when a girl's
voice said, "Hello, Kevin."

Kevin turned and saw Elizabeth Langley. Behind her,
staring in the other direction down Broadway toward the
parade, were her parents.

Kevin froze. His throat tightened. Finally he said,
"Hello, Elizabeth." Even though distracted and upset,
he was struck with how pretty she was with her brown
hair tucked under a small blue bonnet and her gray
eyes. But it wasn't just that she was pretty, he thought.
There was something else about her face, a warmth, a
friendliness. Like her father . . . At that he felt a stab of
pain, and a rush of anger.

"Maureen," he said. "Let's go up Broadway." He added hastily, "You'll see better."

"I see fine now, Kevin." Maureen peered past him. "Who is that?"

"Is that your sister?" Elizabeth asked.

"Yes," Kevin said. He took hold of Maureen's arm. "We have to move up."

"But, Kevin—"

"Hello," Elizabeth said, addressing Maureen. "Your name is Maureen, isn't it?"

"Hello," Maureen said shyly.

"Elizabeth—" Mr. Langley said, turning his head. When he saw Kevin, he stopped. For what seemed to Kevin a long time, he and his former boss stared at one another. Kevin saw he was using a cane. His leg must be better, he thought.

"Kevin—" Mr. Langley started.

Kevin took hold of Maureen's hand. "Come on, Maureen, we have to go." Not looking back at the Langleys he started pulling her through the crowd and toward the front where the policemen were. "We have to cross over."

"But they're coming," Maureen protested. "The marchers, I mean."

"We have time," Kevin said. Still gripping her hand, he dodged between two policemen and ran across the path of the approaching marchers, pulling Maureen after him.

When they reached the other side, Maureen stopped. "Can't we stay here and watch the parade, Kevin?

"No," Kevin said. "Da told me to take you home. And I have to get back to looking for work."

With Maureen still grumbling that she hadn't been allowed to watch the parade, he got her safely home. Then he paused and thought about what to do next. His stomach growled with hunger.

As though in response, Maureen said, "What've we got to eat, Kevin? I'm so hungry!"

He looked in the cupboard, slapping his hand on the shelf to chase away a cockroach also looking for food. But there was none. They'd eaten the last that morning. He put his hand in his pocket. There were two pennies. At least that would buy some bread. "Wait here," he said to Maureen. "I'll get us something."

As he was running down from the third to the second flight, he turned and saw a man coming up the stairs. He stopped. The man looked up and Kevin found himself staring at Timmins's face.

"I've come to collect all the rent," Timmins said. "I've come to get it today, or all of you are out."

Neighbors appeared suddenly. Mrs. Casey from the front apartment on the same floor as the O'Donnells, and Mrs. Scanlan from the floor below stared down the stairwell.

"Ah, leave the poor children alone, Mr. Timmins!" Mrs. Casey said. "Their da's in the hospital. You can't expect them to have the money if he's not here. He'll be back and pay it."

"He didn't pay it before he went in the hospital. And I don't know where he's going to get it now. He's behind in his rent and there are people who want the apartment."

"And you, you greedy man, are going to raise the rent on them so you can collect more money, aren't you?"

"If I run the apartment, then it's my right to get as much for it as I can."

"Me da'll be back next week," Kevin said quickly. "He can pay you then."

"Oh no he won't. From what I hear, he's nowhere near ready to come back. I've made inquiries. And he won't be getting a job on the docks again. Not with his heart."

"You're a terrible man, Mr. Timmins," Mrs. Scanlan shouted down the stairs, "persecuting orphans like this!"

"If O'Donnell is dead and these two are orphans like you say, then they belong in the orphanage." He added piously, "It's illegal to have children living alone."

"But it's all right if they're out on the streets!"

"It's not my job," Timmins started, then stopped. By this time there were women all around the stairwell, their arms on their hips, their faces angry. He was surrounded above and below by angry women.

"I'm coming back tomorrow with a policeman," he shouted up at Kevin, who was peering down the stairs. "And you'll have that money or you and your sister'll be out on the street with your belongings."

"Filthy murderer," one of the women muttered.

"Doesn't care what he does to women and children," another one said. "Doesn't care if they die!"

"I'm sure you have a family of your own, Mr. Timmins," a third women said gently. "And you wouldn't want them turned into the street."

He stared at the circle of faces above and below him, then turned and went down the stairs and out the front door, a chorus of angry comments following him.

Kevin watched as the women went slowly back into their apartments.

"What're you going to do, lad?" Mrs. Scanlan asked. When he didn't reply she added, "Why don't you go see Father Martin? He might have a few dollars for you."

Kevin mumbled something that could be taken for "Yes, I will."

"You do that, lad," Mrs. Scanlan said. "And tonight I'll be having some stew and a bit of pudding for you and your sister."

"Thanks, ma'am," Kevin said. But as he ran down the stairs he knew the last thing he wanted to do was approach Father Martin. Everyone in the neighborhood knew that in dire straits parishioners could go to him for money. If he thought the case was deserving, he would appeal to the bishop, and it was well known that he had found help for families that were starving or on the street. Kevin knew that if he went to him he'd probably get some money from the Church. But not soon enough. Timmons said he'd be back tomorrow. So what was the point?

And one thing he could be sure about was that he'd also get a stern lecture on attending Confirmation classes, as he had before. And if Father Martin thought there was any chance of his and Maureen being left orphans, he, too, would start talking about the Catholic Protectory or the New York Foundling Hospital or the Mission Father Drumgoole, just opened for homeless and destitute children on the corner of Lafayette and Great Jones streets. But that was only for boys. So what would happen to Maureen if Father Martin and the Church had him sent there? What if she hated wherever Father Martin sent her and she ran away? She was only ten, but he'd seen girls no older get into serious trouble.

It was a day he never forgot.

He stopped at every shop, business, and street vendor to see if anyone had a job.

At some point he went to see the tailor. "I'm looking for a job, a steady job. Do you have one?"

The man looked at him. "Not if you can't sew. Remember?" As Kevin stood there he said, "All I have is for you to deliver a letter now and then for a nickel. Is that what you mean?"

Kevin shook his head. Then said, "Got a letter now?"

The tailor stared. "Are you hungry?"

When Kevin nodded, the tailor reached down beside him and brought up a paper parcel, unwrapped it, and lifted out a long and thick sausage. He broke it in two and held half out to Kevin.

Kevin stared. He'd never seen anything like it, nor smelled such a strange, delicious aroma. As the tailor continued to hold it, Kevin reached out for the sausage and took a bite. "That's good!" he said, both delighted and surprised. "What is it?"

"Knackwurst."

Talking around the sausage in his mouth, Kevin tried to pronounce it, then laughed. "What funny words! What language is that?"

The man looked at him. "German. Do you speak any?"

"Me? No. I'm Irish. Are you German?"

"No. I come from Russia. But this kind of sausage is made in Germany and by the German immigrants here in Kleinedeutschland."

Kevin suddenly remembered his boss, Mr. Langley, talking about Kleinedeutschland. The memory both hurt and angered him. He pushed it away. "Was it bad in Russia? Is that why you're here?"

"I was driven out by a pogrom."

"What's that?"

"It's when they kill as many of your people as they can and drive the others out."

"That's awful. 'Course, the English took our land in Ireland and when people were starving in the famine they didn't do anything to help." Quickly he finished the last of the sausage in his hand. Maureen would like this, he thought. "Got any more?" he asked.

"Only what I need for myself."

He considered asking if he could buy it anywhere, but he didn't have any money, anyway. He turned to go. Then, at the door, he looked back. "Thanks. Thanks a lot!"

For the first time since he'd known him, he saw the man smile under his beard.

At the end of the day, he'd looked everywhere and asked everyone and still had no money. The thought of Timmins demanding rent the next day hung over him like a black cloud. Finally, in desperation and braced for the lecture he was sure he'd get, he had gone to St. Catherine's to see Father Martin. But Father Martin was out and no one seemed to know when he'd be back.

Tired and very hungry, he had gone into a big grocery shop on the Bowery that sometimes used him as a messenger, and was waiting to see if they had any work when he saw a coin purse lying on a side counter near the front.

Just like Mrs. Langley's, he thought bitterly. The pain and anger rushed back. Because of her and her purse he'd been accused of stealing. The boss he had come to trust had turned on him. He'd lost his job. A small voice in his head murmured that he'd quit of his own accord, but he pushed it away. After what they'd done he had no choice but to leave. So now he and his sister had no food and would be turned out on the street tomorrow. The rage in him grew.

He looked around. There were two women in the store, each carrying a handbag. Maybe one of them had taken the purse out of her handbag and forgotten to put it back. He loitered in the front, pretending to look at the fruit in the baskets there, but keeping an eye on the women. He knew he could go up with the purse and ask them, but he waited and saw each woman open her handbag, take out a purse, pay for something, then put it back. When they left, talking to each other and not seeing the purse on the side counter, he told himself the purse was lost. For a while he just stared at it.

He had been taught how wrong stealing was, and the priest often delivered sermons on the subject at Mass. Except for the odd penny newspaper, he had never stolen and had never thought of himself as a thief.

But then Kevin thought about Timmins coming tomorrow for the rent and about Maureen having nothing to eat and his failure all day to get her anything. Anger rushed back in him, and with it, desperation.

He looked around again. The store owner had come nearer the front, but had his back turned to Kevin as he sorted through some baskets. Kevin waited. No one came back to reclaim the purse.

He tiptoed over to the counter and looked at the purse. It was fat and covered with beads. Turning his back to the counter, Kevin put his hand behind him and slid the purse off the counter, but it fell onto the floor. Cursing his own clumsiness, he quickly bent, picked it up, and slid it into his pocket. As he tried to sneak out, he heard the owner's voice, "What do you have there?" Kevin ran out of the store and was running as hard as he could to the nearest corner when he heard feet behind him.

"Stop, thief!"

He was aware of people staring at him as he passed.

But he knew he was a fast runner and was just think-ing he was safe, when he saw a policeman in front.

"Hold him!" the man in back of him shouted.

The policeman looked up. Before Kevin could veer away, he found himself confronted.

"And where do you think you're going to, me lad?"

"Nowhere, I'm not going anywhere."

"Hold him!" the store owner behind yelled again. "He stole a purse."

"Did he now?" The policeman got a firm grip on Kevin's collar. He looked him up and down. With his other hand he patted Kevin's pocket. "And what's that you got in there?"

"Nothing."

"I don't think you'd call this nothing."

Before Kevin could make a move the policeman, still holding him by his collar, ran his hand in Kevin's pocket and brought out the purse. He looked at the infuriated store owner behind Kevin. "Is this the purse?"

"It is," the storeowner said angrily "I recognize it. It belongs to one of the ladies who shops in my store all the time." He looked at Kevin. "You little thief! You should be punished!"

The policeman tightened his grip on Kevin's collar. "You can come with me to the precinct and we'll talk about it there."

It took two policemen, tugging Kevin along, to get him to the precinct, where they threw him into the holding cell.

Kevin was not alone in the cell. There were three other men, one asleep on the only bed, which was more like a bench, the two others sitting on the floor. It didn't take long for Kevin to realize they'd both been drinking.

One stared at Kevin out of resentful dark eyes. The other looked him over. "And what are you doing here, lad?"

"Nothing. They're daft."

"What'd he do?" The man suddenly shouted to the copper at the desk. "He's only a kid."

"Nothing!" Kevin shouted.

But the copper drowned him out, saying loudly, "He stole a purse with twenty-three dollars in it from Finley's grocery store." The copper picked it up. "And a fine purse it is. Real leather, with beads. Must have belonged to some lady toff. She'll likely be coming in to claim it. Then we'll know exactly what this fine boyo did."

The policeman walked over to the other side of the bars, twirling his stick. "You want trouble, laddie?"

Kevin stared back.

"Well?"

"I've got a sister at home and there's nobody to take care of her. Me da's in the hospital."

"You should have thought of that sooner." And the copper strolled away.

"Who're you pinching for?" The dark-eyed cell mate said.

Kevin started to deny it again, but suddenly knew it was no use. He pressed his head against the bars and muttered, "Nobody."

"Yeah," the man said, "I bet." After a minute he came over and put his head near Kevin's. "I could get you a job."

Kevin, who'd spent all day and the day before trying to find one, said, "Where?"

"I know some guys who know other guys. They could use a bright lad like you. Only you'd have to stay out of trouble."

"Job doing what?"

"What you're in here for."

"I'm not a thief," Kevin said indignantly.

"No? Well, what you're doing here?"

There was no answer to that. At least not one Kevin wanted to give. He slouched over to the wall of the cell and leaned against it. After a while he slid down to the floor and put his head on his knees.

What would happen to Maureen if he didn't go home? If Timmons came back to the tenement tomorrow as he said he would, what would he do to her—beside throwing out all their belongings? Take her to the Foundling Hospital, or the Children's Aid Society, where she could be shipped out west somewhere and he'd never see her again?

When he thought about his job at the paper and Mr. Langley, the old sadness and anger swept over him, only now the sadness seemed worse. So he tried to concentrate on his anger, dwelling on the injustice his former boss had done to him, not believing him when he said he hadn't taken Mrs. Langley's money.

But he was here because he *had* stolen a purse, a nagging voice reminded him. That's different, he tried to tell himself. But he knew it wasn't.

The hours passed. Even though it was hard on the cell floor, he must have drifted off to sleep. Suddenly he woke up. Someone was shaking him.

"Kevin, Kevin!" He was jolted awake. Staring down at him was Father Martin.

"Father," he mumbled, struggling to his feet.

"Kevin, the policeman tells me you stole twenty-three dollars from a woman in Finley's grocery store!"

Kevin wished he could deny it. But he knew he couldn't. Not to Father Martin. "Yes, Father," he said.

"You know that's wrong, Kevin. I don't have to tell you that!"

Kevin nodded.

"Why did you do it?"

"Da's still in the hospital, Father, and Timmins is coming tomorrow for the rent. He says he'll throw us and our stuff out on the street."

"I see," the priest said slowly. He paused. "It was wrong of you to take the money, of course. But . . . well . . . I wish I could give you the money now, but I don't have it. So many people are badly off. But what about that job you had? It was the *Chronicle,* wasn't it? Do you still have it?"

"No."

"What happened?"

"I'm not going back," Kevin said.

"Why not? It's not going to give you the money for the rent, or to replace what you stole, of course. But you still need the pay for you and Maureen."

When Kevin didn't say anything, Father Martin repeated, "What happened, Kevin?"

"They said I stole some money from a purse Mrs. Langley left on a table. I truly didn't, Father, but they said I did, and . . . and the boss believed them. So I told him he could keep his job."

Father Martin was frowning. "Mrs. Langley? Was this at the office?"

"No, the boss broke his leg, so I go—I had to go up to his house in Washington Square every day taking papers and stuff and he'd dictate and I'd take them back to the paper."

"And Mrs. Langley said you'd stolen from her purse?"

"Yes, at least Christopher, their son, said I did at first. And then she said I did. And when I put my hand in my pocket, the money was there. But I didn't take it, Father. I didn't. I'd never have stolen from Mr. Langley! But he wouldn't believe me."

The priest was silent while he looked into his eyes. Then, "Are you telling me the truth now, Kevin? After all, you've just admitted that you did stole a purse from the grocery store. How can I believe you?"

Kevin looked up into the kindly but piercing brown eyes. "Yes, Father, I am telling you the truth. Honestly!"

Father Martin sighed. "I'll see what I can do. At least I'll speak to the policeman at the desk and explain your circumstance." He looked down at Kevin. "Now try and be a good boy and don't ever steal again! Have they fed you?"

"No, Father." He looked up at the priest. "How did you know I was here?"

"From Tommy Meehan and some of your other friends on Mulberry Street. The word's got around."

"Father, Timmins said he'd be back tomorrow. I don't know what he's going to do to Maureen with me here and Da in the hospital."

"I'll explain that to the sergeant here, too." He patted Kevin on the shoulder. "Now, try and be patient while you have to be here. I'm going over now and speak to him, then I'll go and see if Maureen's all right."

"Father, what are they going to do with me?" When the priest didn't answer, he said, panic in his voice, "Send me to jail?"

"I hope not, Kevin. But it was wrong to steal, though I know why you did. Say a prayer now, and make a good Act of Contrition."

Kevin knelt on the cell's stone floor and bowed his head. After he had said the Act of Contrition the priest made the sign of the cross and spoke the absolution. Then he sighed. "All right, Kevin, I'll see what I can do."

The priest nodded at the two other men, and left.

"So he's going to put in a good word for you?" the dark-eyed one said.

"I hope so," Kevin muttered.

"Maybe you'd better do what the father said," the other man said. "Say a prayer, and while you're doing it, don't forget about us."

Kevin watched as the priest went over and talked to the sergeant. There was too much noise for him to hear what Father Martin was saying. The sergeant didn't show much expression. When he left, Father Martin turned and nodded at Kevin.

It was a long night.

Kevin was awakened the next morning by the sergeant's voice. "Here's some bread."

The crust was stale and hard and less than clean. But Kevin swallowed it ravenously. He looked around hopefully, but the men had eaten their own pieces.

When the sergeant—a different one this time from the one of the night before—came to take away one of the men in the cell, Kevin said to him. "How long are you keeping me?"

"Until a judge says what we're to do with you."

"But I have to get some food for my sister. Me da's in the hospital."

The sergeant looked at him cynically. "You'be surprised how many sad stories I hear about why jailbirds do what they do. It doesn't matter. A theft is a theft. The law's the law."

"What are you going to do with me?"

"Like I said, we're waiting for word from the judge. Then, likely, we'll take you down to the matron at headquarters later—maybe tomorrow."

"No," Kevin cried. "No!" he shouted again as the man walked away.

"So now you don't have to ask again," one of the men in the cell said, and gave Kevin a slight cuff on the head.

Both chilled and hungry, Kevin dozed on and off during the day. The man who'd been lying on the bench was gone, but there were three others, one of them now on the bench, the other two sitting on the floor or standing as the long hours passed.

He thought about Maureen and his job at the paper and Mr. Langley. Finally, and reluctantly, he thought about what he'd done and the sin he'd committed by stealing. Because it was a sin, he knew that as well as the priest did, and if he hadn't made his confession he would be sent to hell. Then he found himself worrying about Mickey, the cat. Would anybody have fed him? Not likely. He'd probably be out on the street now, another casualty of Kevin's sin.

Some time later Kevin was dozing when he heard the clanking of the sergeant's keys in the cell lock. He raised his head. The sergeant was looking down at him and smiling. "You can go now."

Kevin stared, then stood and shot out of the cell, afraid the sergeant might change his mind. He saw a man standing at the desk writing in a book and realized with a shock that it was Mr. Langley.

Mr. Langley turned. "Ready to go, Kevin?"

"What . . . Yes. Sir," he added.

"He's paid a fine for you and got the judge's permission to release you," the sergeant said. "You're a lucky boy!"

Kevin, near tears, couldn't say anything.

"Come along, Kevin," Mr. Langley said. He walked stiffly ahead, using his cane.

When they got outside, he turned to Kevin. "I owe you an apology, Kevin. Elizabeth told me yesterday that she knew you didn't steal the money from my wife's purse. I'm sorry to have doubted you."

Kevin stared. Then he asked, "Why didn't she say so before?"

Mr. Langley took a breath. "It seems that Christopher put the money from his mother's purse into the pockets of your jacket when it was in the hall. Elizabeth saw him do it, but he told her he'd let Thor near Bunny— I'm sure you remember Thor—if she said anything about it."

He paused and then burst out, "I can't tell you how . . . how distressed and angry I am about this. According to my wife, I have only myself to thank. She says I humiliated Christopher in front of you when I made him apologize to you. I still think I was right about that. He was rude and he should have apologized. But, well, it seems, it's obvious that Christopher has problems that I haven't fully understood—including the fact that because he didn't take much interest in the paper, I haven't shown much in him. But that's something else. Again, I'm sorry I misjudged you."

"How . . . how did you know I was here?"

"A priest came to see me. His name was Father Martin. He said he'd seen you here. And he told me you'd stolen the money because you and your sister were going to be evicted."

"The landlord was supposed to come back today."

"He did already. Father Martin told me where you lived. I went there and found Mr. Timmins threatening your little sister." Mr. Langley paused. "He did a lot of blustering about back rent and his duty to send you and your sister to an almshouse. I told him if he tried any such thing I'd put it on the front page of the *Chronicle*." Langley glanced down at Kevin. "There's an election coming up soon, and I don't think the people running—some landlords among them—would want that story spread."

"What did Timmins say?" Kevin asked. His throat was full and he found it hard to talk.

"He backed down."

"But the rent. . . ."

"I paid it. Your father and I can talk about that later. I went to see him in the hospital and told him I knew of a job when he gets out that wouldn't be so hard physically." As Kevin stared, he said, "Now, Kevin, are you coming back to the paper?"

"But do you want me to? I didn't steal from Mrs. Langley's purse"—he gulped and took a breath—"but I did steal the one in the grocery store."

"Stealing is wrong. But given the pressures on you, I might have done the same. Don't do it again, Kevin. You have other resources, believe me!"

Kevin looked down, trying to stem the emotions that threatened to engulf him. After a minute he swallowed and said, "The cat, Mickey, is he out in the street now?"

"No. Did you think I'd put our cat out? He's actually caught a few mice." Langley paused. "To tell you the truth, he now lives at home with me."

Kevin could no longer hold back the tears. Ashamed, he put his hands over his face. In a minute he felt Mr. Langley's hand on his shoulder. "Here's your week's salary, Kevin." He was holding out three dollars.

Kevin couldn't believe that anyone would be that kind. He gulped. "Thank you. Thank you for . . . for everything." He paused, then took a big breath. "Can I have my job back?"

"Yes. You *may* have your job back. By the way, you might be interested to hear we've heard from some of our readers about your letter. Remember what we talked about? About your becoming a journalist? That still holds—*if* you promise me you'll stay in school. Now, are you going to do that, Kevin?"

"Yes," Kevin gulped. "Yes, I will." What he had to say next was the hardest thing he'd ever done. But he knew he had to do it. "I'm sorry . . . sorry I . . . didn't trust you."

"It's all right, Kevin. You had good reason. Trust has to go both ways. I'll see you tomorrow at the paper."